BELONGING

BELONGING

· A NOVEL ·

DEBORAH KENT

The Dial Press / New York

The Dial Press
1 Dag Hammarskjold Plaza
New York, New York 10017

Lines from "anyone lived in a pretty how town . . ."
and "all in green went my love riding . . ."
by e.e. cummings from *Complete Poems: 1913–1962,*
used by permission of Harcourt Brace Jovanovich, Inc.

Library of Congress Cataloging in Publication Data
Kent, Deborah. Belonging.
Summary: Fifteen-year-old Meg realizes that
it's not her blindness that prevents her from joining the
"in" crowd but her own individuality.
[1. Individuality—Fiction.   2. Blind—Fiction.
3. Physically handicapped—Fiction]   I. Title.
PZ7.K413Be   [Fic]   77-14734
ISBN 0-8037-0530-1

*To the Wednesday night group for the inspiration
and to the writers of San Miguel
for the guidance and encouragement without which
this book would never have been written.*

BELONGING

1

I woke to the cardinal whistling in the maple tree outside my window. At that time of year the birds still sang, but only very early in the morning, and I lay listening for a long moment, slowly coming out of my dreams, before I remembered what day it was.

Mom's voice in the hall outside my door suddenly made it all too real. "Meg, are you up yet? It's seven-fifteen."

"I'm up." I tossed back the covers and swung my feet over the edge of the bed.

"Don't rush," she said, opening the door. "You've

got plenty of time." There was worry in her voice. She used to tell me to hurry up, to make it snappy, when I had to catch the bus to the other school.

"I know," I tried to reassure her. "I'm okay."

My velvet skirt and the turtleneck that went with it were folded over the back of my chair. I dressed quickly, my nervous fingers tangling around zipper and buttons. It was hard to concentrate on what I was doing with thoughts of the day ahead churning through my mind.

The cardinal had stopped singing by the time I started on my hair. I wore it in a long ponytail, and for a while I stood at the bureau choosing the right barrette to fasten it today. At last I selected a clover of braided reed from Chinatown in New York. As my fingers traced its delicate twists and curves, I told myself that it would bring me luck.

The kitchen was alive with snapping and sizzling from the stove, and the enticing aroma of bacon floated toward me. "You look lovely," Mom greeted me. I braced myself for one of the suggestions that usually came next: "Just brush the hair back from your face a little," or, "Brush off the front of your skirt, it's got lint on it." But none came. "I fixed a treat for breakfast," she said as I discovered a plate of scrambled eggs and bacon at my place instead of the usual bowl of cold cereal.

And there was hot chocolate too, a big steaming

mug of it instead of the usual cup of tea just beyond the tip of my knife.

My brother, Sam, reached past me to put some bread in the toaster. "I wish Meg started regular school every day if it means we get this kind of breakfast."

"Well, how does it feel?" Dad's morning paper rattled as he turned the page. Dad never started the day without the *Times*. At least something was normal about this morning. "Are you nervous?"

"No, why? There's nothing to be nervous about."

"Man, I'd be nervous if I were you," Sam said. "I wish I'd never have to go to that high school. That place looks awful just from the outside, like some kind of jail or something. And all those millions of kids . . ."

"I can't wait to start," I said. After all, I reminded myself, no one had forced me to do this. It was my own idea.

"You shouldn't have any real trouble," Mom said for about the dozenth time. "You've got all your Braille books now, that's the main thing."

"We're going to give it a try, anyway." Dad threw aside the section he had finished and gave us his full attention. "If it doesn't work out this semester, the Institute really isn't the chamber of horrors you make it out to be."

"It's going to work out," I promised. This was no time to reopen the old debate. We had taken a guided tour of the Institute for the Blind last March, and the director had proudly shown us the facilities. "We have a drama club and a newspaper and a swimming team, just as in a regular high school," she had told us. But I didn't want to go to a place that was just *like* a regular school.

"I wish school didn't ever have to start," Sam stated. He was eleven, four years younger than I was, and entering the sixth grade. "It's the same old junk every year, only every year they give you more homework."

"I'm not looking forward to that part," I said. I was thankful for Sam's presence. Throughout the long weeks of discussion about where I should attend my second year of high school, Sam had been the only member of the family to remain calm. He seldom commented, but I knew he listened to everything that was said. And I was certain where he stood when he banged down his fork one night at supper and exclaimed, "What's everybody fussing about? If Meg says she can do it, she ought to know!"

But it wasn't so easy for Mom and Dad. They didn't exactly want me to go live and study at the Institute for the Blind. They just didn't know what would happen if I attended regular public-school classes for the first time in my life. I didn't know what would happen either, but I had known for as long as I could remember that I wouldn't be happy until I found out.

Dad scraped back his chair and muttered something about rush-hour traffic. Mom followed him to the front door to kiss him good-bye, and for a few moments Sam and I were alone at the table.

"I can walk with you this morning, if you want," he offered.

For a second I wished that he would. I dreaded entering that cavernous building full of strangers! But no one else would arrive this first morning escorted by a little brother. I had to go by myself. "No," I told him, "it'd be out of your way. Thanks anyhow."

The front door slammed and Mom came back into the kitchen. "Have you got everything ready?" she asked.

"What's there to get ready?"

"Well, have you figured out which volumes you need?"

"They're already in my book bag." I opened the refrigerator and found room for the milk pitcher. "They're going to flip out when they see how many volumes it takes for all of my books." I had nine volumes of English grammar, eleven of Spanish, and fourteen of algebra, all patiently transcribed in Braille by volunteers. Each volume was three times the size of an ordinary print book.

On the radio the eight-o'clock news was winding up with the weather report. It was time to go. My folding white cane and my book bag, heavy with Volume One of each of my textbooks, were on the love seat in the den.

"Have you got money for lunch?" Mom asked as she and Sam followed me to the front door. Yes, I had money for lunch. For an awkward moment we all stood in the vestibule discovering that there really was nothing more to say. Then, as though it were an ordinary day, I said a cheerful good-bye, hoisted my book bag, and stepped onto the porch. But on an ordinary day I would have sat down on the wooden bench to wait for the school bus that carried me to the special class for blind children.

I found the first step with the tip of my cane and turned to say a last good-bye. I didn't hear the door shut until I had crossed the lawn to the sidewalk, and I suspected that Mom was watching from the picture window as I turned left and started up Prospect Street on my first walk to school.

It was a sunny September morning, not even jacket weather yet. A light breeze brushed my face, rich with the scent of mown grass and damp earth. Across the street a dog yapped, and English sparrows squabbled in the empty lot next door, as though it were an ordinary day.

I had practiced the walk to school three times the week before with Mom and Sam, and the principal had even given me special permission to enter the building and learn where my classes would be held.

Now, at the corner, I paused to review my directions: left on Prospect to the corner of Willow, across the street and left again down the long hill to Mulberry, across Mulberry, and half a block more to the signpost that marked the entrance to Ridge View High School.

I used to envy Sam his walks to school—friends ringing the doorbell, the group growing larger and noisier as it neared the school yard. From my bench on the front porch I would listen to them, running through piles of dry leaves in the fall, throwing snowballs in the winter, teasing each other and making jokes about their teachers until their voices faded up the street.

The school bus was never like that. I would sit in the corner of my seat, reading a book or losing myself in daydreams, trying to draw away from the hubbub around me. No one had ever said so, but I was always sure that only weird kids had to take a bus and go to a special school. The friends I made there never seemed as good as Sam's friends, who lived in the neighborhood, who could come over after school to play or do homework.

There were voices ahead of me as I walked down the hill, the light, laughing voices of girls my own age. "That's not what she told me," said the one on the right. "She told me he hung up on her."

"Yeah, but Sue, you can never believe what she says. She just likes to go after sympathy."

"I think she was telling the truth," said the one called Sue. Her voice was a little deeper and huskier than her friend's. "She was real upset, crying and all."

Suddenly I was afraid that they would turn and discover me behind them. Had they ever before seen someone who was blind? The rumble of traffic ahead told me that I was nearing Mulberry Street. I tried to tap my cane more lightly, left, right, left, right, assuring me of a clear path in front of me.

The girls had stopped, and I drew up beside them. "Paula's like that, though," Sue's friend said. "She can really put on a big act, and then . . ." She trailed off, and I felt them staring at me. My cane rang against the pavement. The tip dropped down to the street. I put out my foot and found the curb.

"Hi," I said into the silence.

A hand grasped my left wrist. "Careful," said Sue. "This is a real busy street."

"Are you going to school?" I asked as she propelled me forward.

"Yeah. Are you?"

"Yes," I said, and I could think of nothing at all to add. What was Sue thinking, what was she wondering about me? If I could find the right words maybe I could put her at ease, maybe I could restore life to their conversation and it would go on where it had broken off, only now I would be part of it. I would find out about Paula and the boy who hung up on

her. I would make them see that I was just another
fifteen-year-old starting high school today—a little
scared, but everybody was scared, and maybe we were
all really worried about the same things.

"I can walk by myself," I said at the far curb, and
pulled my arm free. For a few moments no one spoke,
and my words echoed in my ears, too harsh, too resentful.

Still, when Sue's friend asked finally, "How are you
going to manage?" I felt a flash of anger.

"Manage what?"

"Oh, you know—getting to classes, and what the
teacher puts on the board—all that stuff."

I was explaining about visiting the school, about my
Braille books, about being able to manage just fine,
when Sue cried, "Darlene! Darlene, you nut, where've
you been all summer?"

Then they were dashing ahead, melting into the
laughing, chattering crowd that swarmed along the
sidewalk. I felt like the only outsider as I pressed into
the throng, alone and silent in the babble of greetings
and gossip, clumsy and conspicuous with my white
cane and my enormous book bag. I wished I had let
Sam come with me after all.

I never found the signpost. As I searched for it
through the crowd my cane tangled among hurrying
feet, and a boy exclaimed, "Why don't you watch
where you're going?" But the signpost was quite un-

necessary. I let the crowd sweep me around the turn, up the walk and through the heavy double front doors of Ridge View High School.

A week ago the corridor had stretched wide and empty, an avenue that lay so straight and clear I longed for a pair of roller skates. I could feel its height and width by the echoes my footsteps set bouncing from the walls and ceiling, and I walked a true course directly down the center. I had known that on this first morning it would not be the same, but nothing had prepared me for this frantic confusion. In the jostling crush of bodies I abandoned the use of my cane and fought ahead with one hand outstretched.

I don't know how I found the stairwell at the end of the hall. A bell rang, and feet thundered around me on the hollow treads. At least, I assured myself, no one had time to stare at me, to notice my uncertain steps and outstretched hand. At least for the moment I was no different from everyone else.

My homeroom, Two Fourteen, was the third door on the right on the second-floor corridor. A week ago I had found it easily by sliding my hand over the tall metal lockers which lined the walls and counting the doorways. But today I couldn't even reach the wall. I counted my steps and listened for clues, but my feet grew more and more unsure. At first I was afraid that I hadn't walked far enough, then that I had passed the door, and at last I seized a shoulder that brushed past me and asked, "Where's Room Two Fourteen?"

"This is Two Twelve right here." It was a girl's voice, thin and nasal, with the hint of a whine.

"I must have passed it then." I turned back, so flustered that I forgot to thank her.

But she followed me protectively. "It must be this one," she said, grasping my arm just above the elbow. "Yeah, Two Fourteen you wanted, right? This is it right here."

"Thanks," I said. I tried to free myself, to enter Two Fourteen firmly on my own this first morning, but her fingers fastened more tightly and she pushed me ahead of her into the room. "I'm okay," I insisted, but she propelled me farther, and I was sure that the eyes of the entire class were fixed upon us.

"Here's a seat for you," she said. Her voice was loud in the relative quiet. "It's the first seat in the first row. That'll be easier for you." Her fingers relaxed their grip; she was gone.

Suddenly I realized that my book bag had grown very heavy. I set it down, folded my cane into its four short sections, and sank onto the hard plastic seat. My heart was pounding, and my hands were clammy with sweat.

A double click from the corner by the door heralded a hollow voice that intoned, "Good morning, students and teachers. This is Mr. Wallace, your principal, welcoming all of you to Ridge View High School. Will everyone now stand to salute the flag."

With a creak of seats the entire roomful of tenth graders rose as one and began, "I pledge allegiance to the flag . . ."

At the head of the first row I wavered, swept by panic. Where was the flag? ". . . of the United States of America . . ." In the Braille class it had hung at the front of the room close to the door. Resolutely I faced straight ahead. ". . . and to the Republic for which it stands. . . ." But in this classroom there must be blackboards running across the front. Then the flag might be on the right side opposite the windows. I turned to the right, not too far, in case the flag was in front after all, but far enough that I might be facing it if it were not. "One nation under God, indivisible, with liberty and justice for all."

As I listened to the introductory speech delivered by Mr. Easton, my homeroom teacher, it became increasingly clear that Ridge View High operated according to a rigid code of regulations. There was to be no smoking, no radios, no eating outside the cafeteria, no gum chewing, no drugs or alcoholic beverages. Boys were not to wear "unbecoming long hair," and girls would be sent home for wearing "immodest skirts." No absence would be excused without a written explanation from parent or guardian. No student would be permitted in the corridors during class time without an official pass from a teacher stating his time of departure and his destination.

"Excuse me, Mr. Easton, but what about . . ." began a boy somewhere in the back.

"If you have a question, first raise your hand and state your name."

"Keith Howard," the questioner obliged. "What are the rules about singing?"

A ripple of laughter played over the room. "Are you a vocalist?" Mr. Easton inquired, and the ripple swelled into a wave, sweeping me along with it.

"Well, I sing sometimes to let off steam," Keith Howard said when the wave had crested and subsided. "It's relaxing."

"I'm sure," said Mr. Easton with professional dignity, "that if your singing interferes with the orderly management of the school, it will be dealt with."

As I traveled from class to class through the morning, the orderly management of the school seemed to be the chief concern of my teachers. In each class I was greeted by a fresh barrage of rules: Textbooks were to be covered, homework was to be handed in on time, lateness was to be penalized. I felt that my blindness was somehow a threat to that order they held so dear. Mrs. Keene, my history teacher, was too nice, detaining me after class with a flurry of questions about what kind of extra help I would need. But Mrs. Gomez, who taught algebra, was openly dismayed. "I was told nothing about this!" she exclaimed. "I don't have time to work with a special student. You should have had algebra in 9th grade! I'm going to discuss this with Mr. Wallace."

Only my English teacher seemed impervious to regulations. "I'm Frances Kellogg," she introduced herself; none of the others admitted to anything so human as a first name. She told us that she didn't like the textbook that the school had supplied, and announced, "I don't care if you never learn any grammar this year. I just want you to start reading."

All in all, it wouldn't have been a bad day if it hadn't been for the cafeteria. Students shouted and shoved, laughed and cursed. All of the regulations of Ridge View High were not enough to establish order there.

"Let me help you." It was a girl's voice, light and friendly. Gratitude overcame my desire for independence, and I was glad to let her maneuver me through the crowd. "Here's the end of the line," she said. "I've already got my tray, or I'd go through it with you. Can you make it from here?"

"Sure. Thanks."

Ahead of me two boys were deep in a discussion of the football team, and I followed them closely as the line crept forward. At last I heard the clatter of silverware just ahead. I found the stack of plastic trays, still hot and moist from recent washing, and hunted for the bins of knives and forks. "Come on! Move it!" a girl grumbled behind me. I grabbed a handful of silverware and slid my tray along the track.

"Hey," I said to the boy ahead of me, "can you tell me what there is here to eat?"

"All kinds of slop. You don't want any." His tray moved on and I followed, wondering miserably what I was passing up. The hiss of frying and the cloud of steam wafting from behind the counter told me we had reached the hot section. "Gimme some of that," the boy said, and I knew that I was next.

"What do you want?" the thin, cracked voice of an elderly woman demanded.

"I . . . I don't know. What is there?"

There was a moment of stunned silence before she burst out, "Oh, I'm so sorry, honey! I didn't realize! You like succotash? Let me give you some of this nice succotash. And how about some chicken croquettes? I'll give you a couple extra. I'm so sorry!"

But the worst part of all was still to come. At the cash register I realized that I still had to find a seat. The boys had dashed ahead, and I had lost their voices in the din. I thought of asking the girl behind me for help, but when I remembered her rough impatience I determined to go on alone. Hoisting my tray with one hand and wielding my cane with the other, I abandoned the safety of the line and entered the dining room.

"Is there an empty seat here?" I asked of anyone who might listen when my cane encountered a table leg.

"No," was the concise reply. Waxed paper rattled, a fork scraped a plate. I stood indecisively, taking in the sounds around me, trying to guess which way I should go. "There's a seat over there," a boy said finally.

"Over where?"

"Right over there. Over there on your left."

"Thanks." I made a sharp left turn and had taken two steps when the collision occurred. The tray leaped from my grasp, and I went down to shouts and the sound of shattering crockery. Inevitably someone cried, "Are you hurt?" and several demanded, "What happened?" Dazed and wretched, I sat on the floor amid the ruins of my lunch and my pride.

"Well," Dad asked at the dinner table, "how was your big day?"

"Fine," I said, and then, in case he might not believe me, "It was a little rough at first with so many kids."

"Did you get a lot of homework?" Sam wanted to know.

"Tons! I never got this much last year."

"Do you need me to read anything to you?" Mom asked.

"No, I'm okay. I even got started in study hall. Everything is working out fine." I paused, remembering the girls on the street, the girl who had helped me find Room Two Fourteen, Mrs. Keene and her anxious questions. "I just wish everybody'd quit trying to be so darn helpful all the time."

"They don't know what you can do and what you can't do," Dad said. "You're going to have to educate them."

"But they really bug me, you know," I said. "I can understand the kids maybe, but you'd think the teachers at least would be a little smarter."

"You'll just have to be patient," Mom said. As usual, she sided with Dad. "They've never known anyone before who was blind, and they're just trying to be nice."

"Nice!" I grumbled. Of course Dad and Mom were probably right, but that still didn't make it any easier. Only in the cafeteria, when I really did need someone, had no one offered assistance, and I had been too proud to ask. Maybe I was expecting people to read my mind.

"I've got the meanest math teacher," Sam said. "She's giving us twenty examples every night!"

"My history teacher's giving us a quiz every Friday,"

I said with a certain pride. "And in English we have to write a composition every week."

When dinner was over I followed Mom into the kitchen and started rinsing the plates. For a while we worked together in silence, putting the food away and loading the dishwasher. So I was caught off guard when she asked with sudden urgency, "How do you really feel about school?"

"I'm glad I'm there," I said. There was a lot I wasn't telling her, but that much, at least, was true.

2

If Mrs. Keene hadn't insisted that I be assigned the first seat in the first row, I might never have gotten to know Jeffrey Allen. Seating was alphabetical, and as my last name was Hollis, I belonged back among the H's. "But it will be so much easier for you to sit in front right by the door," Mrs. Keene explained. I had not yet discovered Jeffrey Allen; I protested. But she was the teacher. I got the first seat in the first row, and Jeffrey Allen sat right behind me.

It was his voice that I noticed first. A lot of the boys still spoke in squeaky trebles, some were at that hoarse, in-between stage, but Jeffrey's voice had already achieved the deep resonance of manhood. Even his simple "Here!" when Mrs. Keene called the roll thrilled me strangely with its ring of masculine confidence.

He never volunteered an answer in class, but he talked a lot every morning, before the bell rang, to a boy named Warren who sat across the aisle. They talked about Jeffrey's standing on the soccer team (the school paper had hailed him as this year's most promising sophomore), and his campaign for Sophomore Class Treasurer. Once he told Warren he had almost been caught smoking in the boys' room that morning. He hadn't been scared, he said; it was all very funny, and he described how the janitor had come in, sniffing suspiciously. I felt invisible where I sat in front of him, sharing the excitement, laughing secretly to myself.

I found myself making up stories about him in boring classes, on long drives with the family, through sermons on Sundays. Sometimes Jeffrey asked me to help him write campaign slogans; sometimes he invited me to join him for lunch; and in one of my favorites I discovered that his family was going to build a house on the empty lot next door to us.

But again it was Mrs. Keene who actually brought us together. In an otherwise quite ordinary class during the third week of school, she suddenly announced that she was assigning a special project to each row.

We would have a week to prepare a presentation to the rest of the class. The first row was assigned "The Pyramids of Egypt."

There were five of us: Jeffrey and myself, a girl named Karen Cardelli, and two boys called Peter and Bruce. During the last ten minutes of the class period we gathered in a corner of the room, shouting above the babble of four other simultaneous meetings. The boys exchanged a few suggestions, the most popular of which was the mummification of Mrs. Keene, and Karen leafed through the history book, reading aloud the chapter headings in a vague attempt at research. I was still invisible.

This was my chance. Today I was going to make Jeffrey notice me. "I think we ought to have a chairman," I stated, my heart racing.

"Or woman." I wasn't sure if it was Bruce or Peter; their voices were dismayingly alike. "Let's see the girls do some work around here."

"It was Meg's idea," Jeffrey said. "Let her be the chairperson if she wants."

"Anybody can do it. I didn't mean it had to be me," I protested. But I had no will to dispute an honor which Jeffrey bestowed upon me. I spent the rest of the day just remembering the way he said my name.

I quickly discovered that my position accorded me very little honor but plenty of work. As the days passed, the boys settled back to accept whatever help Karen and I offered them. Nothing was getting done, and the day of the presentation, Tuesday, rushed nearer and nearer. At last, on Friday, I suggested to Karen that we meet in the school library to do the necessary reading.

I got there a few minutes past three. Somehow I didn't want to call Karen's name into the silence in front of me. I didn't want to stand in the doorway either, lost and forlorn, waiting for her to notice me. I stepped deeper into the room, exploring ahead of me with my cane to find tables and chairs.

"Meg!" I whirled. Karen's feet tapped toward me across the floor. "Hi, I just got here. Look out, there's a table right in front of you. You want a chair? Here's a chair."

I accepted and sat down. I set my Braille writer on the table and rolled in a sheet of paper. Karen still stood beside me, watching curiously.

"How come it's only got six keys and there are twenty-six letters?" she asked at last.

"Because Braille only uses six dots," I explained. If I could answer her questions, then maybe we could go on to other things. I could find out what sort of person she was, I could tell her about things that really interested me. "All of the letters are made of combinations of the six dots. You press two or three or four or five keys at once, like this."

I wrote the alphabet across the top line, and Karen touched it curiously. "They all feel the same to me," she said. "I don't know how you do it."

"I've just been doing it since kindergarten," I told her. "I guess I'm used to it. Hey, let's get going on the pyramids."

"I don't know where to start, do you?"

"Well, let's look in the card catalog."

Karen didn't seem to know where the card catalog was, or how to use it once it was found. I asked her to read me the titles listed under *Egypt*, selected two, and sat down to take notes while she read aloud. By four o'clock I thought we had gathered enough information for a ten-minute presentation. "I'll type up the notes so everybody can read them," I promised. We were both relieved to call it a day.

"I still don't see how you can read this." She ran her hand over a page of Braille in my looseleaf notebook. "It just feels like bumps."

"Where do you live?" I asked. I'd been reading and writing Braille for so long it wasn't especially interesting to me.

"Over on Willow Court. That's way the other side of town. I usually catch the school bus, but today I guess I'm walking. How about you?"

"Just a couple of blocks away." I unfolded my cane. Its four sections snapped together with the force of the elastic that runs through the middle to connect them. I knew that Karen was marveling again, but I went on, "Let's get those boys to do some of the work. If we tell them what to say, they can at least help in the presentation."

"Do you want me to help you somewhere?" We had started for the door.

"No, I'm fine. Really." I maneuvered between two tables. "Don't worry about me."

"It's just I keep on thinking"—she took hold of my arm—"I keep thinking, how would I do it? I mean, if I couldn't see, I wouldn't know how to do anything."

"You'd learn." What did other girls talk about? "Isn't Mrs. Keene a drag? Don't you get so bored?"

She didn't answer. Her attention seemed to have been caught by someone or something in the hall ahead of us. "Jeffrey!" she called, and my knees began to tremble. "How's it going?"

"What are you doing, hanging out here so late?" It was Jeffrey all right, turning, coming toward us.

"We were in the library," I began, "working on that thing for history. . . ."

"Oh, just grinding away," Karen said above my words. "Hey, tell me, how did that thing work out this afternoon?"

"Oh that. Right. It's all okay. Everything's set."

"Great!" For the first time that afternoon Karen's voice bubbled with fun. "I knew you'd pull it off."

"Listen," Jeffrey said. He was so close I could have

touched him. I could sense the height of his figure beside me, could smell sweat mingled with the starched smell of his shirt. "You want to go for a ride? Kevin's out front with the car."

"Out of sight! I just missed the bus, and I wasn't really up for walking." Karen still held my arm as we crossed the foyer. I ought to slip away gracefully somehow. I hadn't been invited, or even acknowledged. But maybe it was just understood that I was going with them, maybe it didn't have to be said—and we passed through the double doors and down the front steps.

"I wish we had more room," Jeffrey said, turning to me. "My brother's got a little Triumph. It only seats three. You can get home okay?"

"Sure," I told him, forcing a smile. Karen let go of my arm. "See you in class Monday."

Somewhere someone was burning leaves. I took a deep breath and let the rich fall smell fill my head, let it blot out the feelings that rose and threatened to take hold of me.

" 'Bye!" they called. A few yards away an engine purred, and they hurried toward it while I turned and started home.

The presentation was a success. Each of us spoke for two or three minutes. When it was all over and Mrs. Keene had awarded us a B plus, Jeffrey leaned toward me and touched my hand. "Thanks, chairperson," he said. "I always knew you were smart."

For long tingling minutes afterward I felt the warm imprint of his fingers across the back of my hand, and nothing else was important. After all, his brother's Triumph only seated three, and Karen had a longer walk home than I had. I spent the rest of that class period indulging in a whole new set of fantasies, all about after-school study sessions together that led to tender words and gentle touches, to an ever-deepening friendship.

The bell jarred me back to the world. The door opened, flooding the room with noise from the corridor, and the class swirled into life. There were only four minutes allotted between classes, barely time for a stop at locker or washroom.

"Well, can you make it?" Karen spoke so close to my ear that for a moment I thought she was talking to me.

Then Jeffrey answered, slowly, considering. "Saturday night? Sure, I guess so. Am I supposed to bring something or what?"

"Oh, if you want. It's just a plain old party." She giggled. "Just the usual bunch coming over to hang out in the basement and—you know. . . ."

"Will your mother be home?" Jeffrey asked. I rearranged my books, checked again that my algebra homework was tucked into the front of my notebook.

"Yeah, but she never comes down." They laughed together, as though they shared a secret. "Hey," she said, "I've got to run. Be seeing you."

"Right," Jeffrey said. "Be seeing you."

I couldn't remember ever feeling quite like this before. This was not the dull longing I had felt, listening to shouts and laughter as I sat on the front porch, yearning for things I knew must exist somewhere but could hardly describe to myself. This feeling sharpened my senses, set me tingling, aching but intensely alive. I didn't realize, in those first moments, that I was wracked by jealousy.

As the day wore on, a few clear thoughts began to emerge. Why couldn't I be having a party, daring to invite someone like Jeffrey? What would happen if I asked him to a party at my house—would he say no outright, or would he accept politely and give an excuse later on? What did Karen Cardelli have that I was lacking?

The bell rang, but no one in Miss Kellogg's class seemed to notice. I could hear her at her desk, opening and shutting drawers as though she were searching for something. At last, over the jumble of conversations, she began: "anyone lived in a pretty how town with up so floating many bells down . . ."

Her voice was neither young nor old, and was tinged with an accent I associated with New England. Slowly the room grew quiet, and by the time the poem drew to a close everyone was listening.

It didn't make any sense to me at first. Her voice poured joy into some lines, sadness into others, but the words themselves told me nothing. Around me there was a restless shuffling, and nervous giggles dotted the room.

"It's like 'Jabberwocky,' " Karen said a few seats behind me. "It doesn't mean anything."

So Miss Kellogg read it again, a second and a third time, pausing to let each line reach us, to give us time to respond. Very slowly, though I couldn't be sure, I felt a glimmer of understanding. Even my jealousy was pushed aside by my struggle to grasp the meaning of the poem.

When she read: "they sowed their isn't they reaped their same." I leaned forward in my seat, and she stopped as though aware of my excitement.

"Meg?" she asked, though I hadn't dared to raise my hand.

"He's saying you get back what you put in, right? If you sow isn'ts, nothing grows but isn'ts."

"I think so," she said. I felt a glow of pleasure. For the first time something I was studying in school seemed related to life.

Before I could sink back into my preoccupation with Karen and Jeffrey, Miss Kellogg made her announcement about the *Messenger*. "It's the school literary magazine," she explained. "I'm supervising it this year. Anybody who'd like to help out can come to this room today at three-fifteen."

Somehow anything that involved Miss Kellogg promised to be exciting, and the prospect of working with her on such a project filled me with anticipation. For a little while, at least, I felt like myself again.

So I was among the dozen or so who assembled in Room Two Thirty-four that afternoon to await Miss Kellogg's arrival. "She probably forgot about the meeting," said a girl beside me. "She's a good teacher, but she sure is scatterbrained."

"Maybe she's just got more important things to think about." Even the hint of criticism was enough to rouse me to Miss Kellogg's defense.

"She does," the girl agreed. "She's too intelligent for this place. She must go nuts around here."

There was a sudden hush, and I knew even before she spoke that Miss Kellogg had come in. "Well," she began, "I never expected such a big turnout. How many of you worked on the *Messenger* last year?"

The show of hands must have been substantial. "I hope you're not going to be too disappointed," she went on. "This is my first year teaching at Ridge View, and I've got a few ideas I'd like to try out. Look at this." She paused, apparently holding up some object for inspection. "I've been looking over a couple of last year's issues. They're a real hodgepodge—jokes, a little reporting on school events, a gossip column, and a poem buried here and there."

She continued, disregarding the indignant murmur that followed her words. "It seems to me that the *Messenger* isn't really a newspaper, and it's not quite a magazine—it's a little of everything, trying to please everybody." I could hear her New England accent for sure in the way she said *Messenjah*.

"This school has no outlet for people with talent in creative writing. There's plenty of recognition for football players and baton twirlers—I've got nothing against that, but I'd like to see more opportunities for other people too. There must be people in this school who write stories and poetry we could publish. So that's why I'd like the *Messenger* to become a real literary magazine this year."

"Who's going to read it?" a boy demanded, giving voice to the general discontent.

"We'll have to find out," Miss Kellogg countered.

"Nobody'll even give us anything to print," a girl muttered.

"I bet people will." It was the girl sitting next to me, the one who had said Miss Kellogg was scatter-brained. "I bet there are people right here in this room who write things and never show anybody."

No, I wanted to tell her, that couldn't be true. Nobody did that but me.

"If we keep worrying what the rest of the school

will think, we'll never do anything." It was a boy's voice, vaguely familiar with its uneven breaking tenor. "Let's just go ahead and see what happens."

"Let's get down to business," Miss Kellogg said, closing the discussion. "First let me get all your names." I learned that the boy whose voice had been familiar was Keith Howard, who had asked for the rules about singing that first morning. The girl sitting next to me was named Lindy Blake.

There were a few who walked out, and a few who grumbled but stayed. But among the rest of us I felt a real bond of enthusiasm. I volunteered to compose a letter to all of the English teachers. We would ask them to encourage their students to submit poems, stories, and essays. It didn't sound like work; it would be my first contribution. I had pictured something like this when I had dreamed of attending public school—the sense of belonging to a group, working as an equal with the others toward a shared goal. And as though that were not enough, I would be working with Miss Kellogg too.

"What do you think so far?" On our way out of the meeting Lindy stopped me with a light touch on my arm.

"It's going to be fun!"

"Well, I think it'll be interesting, anyway," she said. "I'd like to see us really put together something good, just to stir this place up a little."

"How's a literary magazine supposed to do that?" We started down the hall. Without thinking about it, I rested my hand easily in the crook of Lindy's elbow. She was shorter than I was—her head seemed to come only to my chin—and her arm felt thin under her corduroy jacket.

"Nobody even thinks we could get something like that together. The kids who run everything get the rest of us to think we're weird if we want to try something new." She paused. "You didn't go to Ridge View last year, did you?"

To me the question sounded like an accusation. "No," I said warily. "I went to school out of town."

"Private school?" she pursued.

"No, it was public, really." After a moment I went on, "It was a special class, they call it a Braille class. There aren't very many blind kids from this area, so they have all the grades in one room, from kindergarten to ninth. Even then there were only ten of us last year."

"Wow! This place must boggle your mind!"

"There's a lot to get used to," I conceded.

"What do you think of it so far?"

"Well, it's big and crowded—and there sure are a lot of rules!"

"My history teacher actually gave us a quiz on the School Handbook last week," Lindy said. "All that junk about the procedures for going to the bathroom, and which stairways go up and which ones go down. . . ."

"I used to think that was only in books," I said, and we both laughed. "I'll never get it all straight."

Lindy stopped to zip her jacket. "They won't expect you to, I bet."

"Why not?" I demanded. I didn't want her to be right, but she had perceived something I had refused to admit to myself.

"You're enough different they won't know what to do about you. They'll expect you to be good and quiet, but"—a mischievous sparkle crept into her voice—"you could get away with murder."

"I don't want to get away with anything," I quickly protested. "I just want to be treated like everybody else."

"Well, take it from me, you wouldn't like it."

I caught the changes in the echoes around us as the hall widened into the foyer. The rubber doormat was beneath my feet. "Which way do you go to get home?" Lindy asked.

"Up the hill. I live on Prospect."

"Oh. I go the other way, through the center of town. It's kind of far, but I've got my bike."

"But nobody rides . . ." I began, only to amend hastily, "I mean, not many people ride a bike to school, do they?"

"It's definitely uncool," she agreed. "I may as well

tell you the rest—the real reason I ride my bike to school is because I've got a morning paper route."

"I never heard of a girl . . ."

"They wouldn't have given it to me, but I inherited it when my brother went away to college. I guess it's even more uncool than riding a bike. Listen, I'll see you tomorrow. We're in the same English class, you know."

"So long." I heard her unfasten the chain and raise the stand with a kick; she parked her bike right in front of the school, in plain view.

She rang her bicycle bell in farewell as I turned left and started for the corner. Already I knew that I liked her, but I wished that she were a little more like other people.

I was alone for the first time all day as I started up the hill, and my thoughts naturally turned back to Jeffrey Allen. Perhaps this afternoon he had stayed for soccer practice. Now he would just be going home. He would spot me ahead of him and call, "Wait up, Meg! I'll walk with you!" People could stare at me all they wanted if I was walking with Jeffrey; I would be proud. They would look at me with respect, the girls with envy. "Boy," he would say, "that Karen Cardelli, I can't stand that girl! Help me think of an excuse to get out of going to her party."

Behind me I heard a sudden burst of song.

It was so startling to hear someone singing on the

street, full-throated and unashamed, that I stopped in amazement. The music was unfamiliar, and as the singer came nearer I realized that the words were not in English. Even before he spoke, I knew that it had to be Keith Howard.

"Meg!" He broke off at the bottom of a long cascade of notes. "Do you want any help with that letter about the contributions?"

"No," I said quickly, "I don't think so. I can dash something off tonight."

"Oh." His voice lost a little of its luster. "I thought maybe I could help. . . ."

"What were you singing just now?"

"Oh, that? It's from *Siegfried*. It's the part where Siegfried wants to tell . . ."

"Zeeg what?"

"Oh, you don't know opera. *Siegfried*. One of the operas in *The Ring of the Nibelungen*—it's Wagner. The whole story's very complicated, but in this part, Siegfried is telling . . ."

"Don't people look at you kind of funny when you sing like that?" I tried to say it lightly, with a little laugh as though it didn't matter, but I didn't want to stand on the sidewalk with Keith Howard. I wanted to hurry up the hill and close the front door behind me before anyone could see us.

"Oh sure. It's weird and all that. But it's fun, though."

"I have to get home," I said. "They don't expect me to be this late."

But he followed me, still talking. "You ought to listen to the *Ring* cycle sometime. You wouldn't have to listen to it all in one sitting, it's way too long. I'll lend you the records, and I can read you some of the explanations in the booklet that comes with it, okay?"

"Sure," I said. "That'd be nice." I had reached the corner. "Listen, this is where I turn. So long now."

" 'Bye." I didn't want to hear the disappointment that quivered through that single word. A car passed slowly—perhaps Jeffrey sat in the front seat beside his brother, or Karen leaned to stare from the back window. I wanted only to escape from the boy who sang opera on the street.

3

The morning started badly. I mislaid the homework I had labored over for Mrs. Gomez the night before, and spent so long hunting for it that I left for school ten minutes late. Mom noticed my distress and insisted on knowing what was wrong.

"I'd like to have a talk with that algebra teacher," she stated. "I don't know how to help you with math homework. I don't think it would be too much to ask her to give you a little extra . . ."

"Mother, no!" I burst out. "I'm getting it done, please don't worry. . . ."

"You're spending too much time on homework," she said. "Last night I heard you up past eleven o'clock. You're going to get sick if you don't get enough sleep."

"I'm going to be late," I said. "There isn't time to talk about this now. Please don't worry about me!"

But all morning I couldn't thrust away my apprehension. With the best of intentions, Mom might very well make an appointment to talk to Mrs. Gomez. Already I was sure that Mrs. Gomez resented my presence in her class, and I knew that I didn't like her. She was a teacher of the old school, maintaining rigid discipline with her cold voice and, people said, with the dagger looks she could direct at any student who displeased her.

As promised, she had discussed my case with Mr. Wallace, the principal, but he had failed to rescue us from one another. As she leaped from chapter to chapter, from sets to binomials to square roots, I dropped further and further behind the rest of the class. Afraid to call attention to myself by asking questions, I longed only to remain unnoticed. A talk with Mom, as anxious as she was, would just remind Mrs. Gomez of my intrusion into her routine, and was bound to make her more irritable than ever.

Before homeroom period the door of my locker jammed, and a janitor had to be summoned to hammer it open. Naturally the man who arrived on the scene was the same janitor who had mopped up my succotash that first day in the cafeteria. "Always glad to help you out," he said over and over. "Anything you ever need, you just let me know, you hear?"

Be patient, Mom would have said. After all, he was trying to be kind. But nevertheless a wave of anger surged through me. He would not have been so solicitous of anyone else; probably he would have been annoyed, even accusing. I didn't need his kindness if it was offered only because I was blind.

Jeffrey breezed into history class without a word to me, and launched immediately into an involved discussion with Warren across the aisle about something the soccer coach had said yesterday afternoon. Karen was just intruding with the version of the story she had heard from someone else when the bell rang. Mrs. Keene showed a series of slides depicting ruins in the Near East, and as the projector hummed and clicked I nursed my jealousy into a raging blaze.

But Mrs. Gomez's class was next and it was bad policy to be inattentive there. I needed total concentration to hold in my mind the examples she wrote on the blackboard. She read each step aloud only once. Throughout the class period she called on the unsuspecting and the unprepared, requesting them to demonstrate their knowledge.

For me, algebra class was like one of those TV mysteries designed so that you can never grasp the plot if you miss the first five minutes. Ironically it was my concern about Mom's impending conference with Mrs. Gomez that made me lose those critical opening minutes today. I could hear Mom's voice, earnest, pleading even: "It's very important that she do well. You can explain math to Meg better than I can. . . ." And Mrs. Gomez cutting her short, "But I've already explained to you, Mrs. Hollis, that I say each step aloud in class. If the others can follow, then Meg should be able to. . . ."

"Meg!" My name burst out at me from a maze of letters and numbers.

"Pardon?" I managed. "Could you repeat the question, please?"

"I'll repeat it once more." Mrs. Gomez's voice was flat, humorless. "Four XY times six Y?"

It was better to guess than to admit that I didn't know. "Twenty-four XY?"

"Are you asking or telling me?"

I was stepping into a trap. "Telling. Twenty-four XY."

"George, can you help Meg out?"

I tried to focus on the explanation of my error, but another hurdle loomed ahead. I had already rehearsed the scene three times in my head when Mrs. Gomez ordered, "Pass your homework forward."

"I did mine, but I couldn't find it this morning." I lifted imploring, empty hands. "I'll do it again tonight."

"Report to me after class," she said. She crossed the room, stopping at her desk to tap together the stacks of papers she had collected from each row.

Ordinarily the ringing of the bell was a signal of release. This morning it set my heart lurching, and my legs wobbled as I advanced to the front of the room. I felt strangely apart from my classmates, whose glad voices surged toward the door while my outstretched hand sought the edge of Mrs. Gomez's desk.

"You seem to be having some difficulty lately," she began. "You haven't been paying attention or working very hard."

"It's just that I don't always understand . . ." My voice echoed eerily in the empty room.

"I just want you to understand this," she said. "I am not going to be lenient with you because of your handicap. If you don't earn a passing grade, I will not give you a passing grade."

Now it was Dad's voice that broke into my consciousness. "We'll try it for a semester. If it doesn't work out . . ."

"I guess I just need to keep at it."

"I hope you haven't expected any special considerations from me. If you're in my class, you're going to be treated like all the rest of my students."

"Of course," I protested. "I don't want you to treat me differently." But I could hear Dad saying, "If it doesn't work out . . ."

"Well," Lindy reminded me, "you said you wanted to be treated just like everybody else."

"And you said I wouldn't like it." We had eaten lunch together, and had just carried our empty trays to the proper counter. In ten minutes the bell would send us dashing up to Room Two Thirty-four and Miss Kellogg.

"I wish I could go up to my locker now," Lindy said. "I never have time once the mob is turned loose."

"What do you think would happen if we sneaked up there now?" I asked.

Lindy thought a moment. "Let's try it. There's got to be a way we can beat the system."

It was easy enough to step unobserved through the swinging door out of the tumult of the cafeteria into the astounding silence of the empty corridor. We spoke only in whispers as we tiptoed upstairs, meeting no one. By the time we reached Lindy's locker, we both felt safe.

"How old do you think Miss Kellogg is?" I asked as Lindy fiddled with the padlock.

"Hard to say. Thirty, thirty-five maybe. You can't tell, the way she dresses. She doesn't wear any makeup, and some of her clothes kind of hang on her. You can tell that kind of thing isn't important to her."

"I guess not." But after a lifetime of Mom's insistence on the importance of looking nice, I couldn't quite convince myself that Miss Kellogg's indifference was really all right.

Lindy's locker door clanged open at last, releasing a cascade of books that tumbled and thumped to the floor. I stooped to help her gather them up, and it was then, as we crouched on the linoleum, that we heard the footsteps.

They were firm, ominous footsteps, echoing through the stillness. With no possible escape, we rose to face the inquisition.

"Do you girls have passes?"

The voice was not quite as hollow and resonant as the one that greeted us each morning over the public-address system, but I couldn't fail to recognize it.

"Hi, Mr. Wallace," Lindy said brightly, slipping her arm through mine. She talked fast. "We came up early from lunch because Meg has to get the next volume of her English book out of her locker, and the teacher on lunch duty was too busy to write us a pass."

"Oh, I'm sorry." He sounded a little embarrassed. "I just didn't recognize you for a minute." He seized my free hand and gripped it tightly. He smelled faintly of after-shave lotion and cigars. "You know, I haven't had a chance to talk to you since school started, but I've been wanting to tell you how much I admire you. It's impressive, the way you get around; people can hardly tell you're—you're—operating under a handicap."

Why is it so hard for people to say the word *blind*, I wondered, shifting from one foot to the other. Oblivious to my discomfort he went on, "It must be a little rough for you when you have to stop off at your locker and then rush to your next class. Tell you what. I'll write you out a permanent pass. That way, if you need to come up early from lunch for any reason, the teacher on hall patrol won't be concerned."

"Oh, I don't really . . ." I began, but Lindy nudged me and interrupted. "That would really help a lot, wouldn't it, Meg?"

Mr. Wallace's attention shifted to her. "You've been helping her out, is that it? Very nice of you. I'm sure Meg appreciates it. Why don't I put your name on the pass too, just so there won't be any problem. You're . . ."

"Rosalind Blake."

Mr. Wallace released my hand. His pen scratched on a pad. "There." He pressed a slip of paper into my hand. "Hold on to this, and if anyone questions you, send them to me."

"Thanks." My fingers closed around the pass, crumpling it against my palm.

"Now do you see what I mean?" I demanded as his steps faded down the hall. "Do you see why I want to be treated like everybody else?"

"Kind of." Lindy was silent a moment. "Only it's not that they shouldn't give you all those special privileges because you're blind—they ought to be that nice to everybody else, too."

"Well," I said, "since Mr. Wallace isn't about to let everybody else come up early from lunch, I guess I can't do it either." I sensed that Lindy was a little disappointed when I tore the pass in two and dropped it into a waste can at the elbow in the corridor, but she didn't protest. Perhaps, I thought, she was beginning to understand.

The bell rang. All up and down the corridor doors burst open, releasing a babbling, shoving torrent. "Hey, listen," Lindy called to me above the din, "this Saturday you want to go on a hike?"

"But you really don't even know where you're going?" Sam demanded, coming into the kitchen. "Why's it got to be a secret?"

"I wish I knew." But Lindy had been adamant. She wouldn't give me even a hint, and she seemed to take impish delight in my mounting curiosity.

It was far enough away that we were packing a picnic, and I had agreed to make sandwiches. There were two loaves in the bread box—white, large and light; and rye, smaller, denser, and heavier. I took four slices from each and spread them with butter until I could feel no more lumps with the knife blade. I found the peanut butter in the cupboard, a tall jar with a familiar pattern of parallel raised lines. In the refrigerator were two nearly identical jars, one of which had to be the strawberry jelly. I twisted off the lid of the first one and sniffed the contents. Mayonnaise.

"It could be the reservoir," Sam said. I cut the sandwiches and slipped them into a plastic bag. "That'd be about an hour's walk, wouldn't it?"

I had the feeling he wanted me to ask him to come, but I pretended not to notice. This was a special day that I was going to spend with Lindy, and I didn't need my little brother tagging along.

The sandwiches made, I could do nothing but wait. I wandered across the backyard and leaned on the split-rail fence by the garden. A crisp October breeze rustled dry leaves across the lawn. The last of the summer birds had departed, but the empty lot was loud with blue jays and grackles, and in the distance I heard the sharp single note of a nuthatch, its winter call.

Lindy greeted me with two short rings of her bicycle bell, and I ran to meet her at the driveway. "Did you make the sandwiches?" she asked. She ground to a stop, dragging her feet on the asphalt.

I held up the bulging bag. "Come on, tell me where we're going."

But Lindy remained evasive. "You'll see." She snapped her padlock into place. "I can't explain it, I'll just have to show you."

At first I tried to keep careful track of where we

were going, noting to myself each turn and street crossing while we chattered about a book I was reading called *The Once and Future King,* and about a collage she wanted to make out of autumn leaves. But within six blocks of home we turned onto an unfamiliar street, and in ten minutes more we were out on a dirt road, treacherous with potholes. Branches overhead sighed in the wind.

"We're almost there," Lindy said, and we fell silent for the last stretch of the journey, the climb up a steep hill, the turn off the road to cross a rocky stubble field, until at last she put my hand on a pitted wooden post and announced, "This used to be the gate."

"To what?" I demanded.

"To the graveyard."

"The graveyard!" I should have felt a prickle of fright run up my spine, should have felt my scalp tingle as my hair rose to stand on end. But there was no smell of death, only the fragrance of leaf mold. There was no rattle of dry bones, only the distant clamor of a flock of crows and the rasp of a grasshopper almost underfoot.

"Look!" Lindy led me scrambling over fallen branches and scattered rocks to show me a smooth marble slab set at an angle in the ground. The left edge was badly chipped, but my fingers easily traced the carved letters: OHN PETER BOYLE, and below them the dates: 1810–1891.

"It must be John," I said. "He lived to be eighty-one."

"There are lots more," Lindy said. She talked even more quickly than usual in her excitement. "Any way you go you'll find them."

I took a few cautious steps and found another stone with my right foot. In addition to the name, ELIZA-BETH CARGILL, BELOVED WIFE, it bore a worn relief of two plump cherubs.

"They don't use this graveyard anymore," Lindy explained. "Maybe it got too crowded, or maybe people just wanted to get buried in a fancy place with a care-taker to mow the lawn and plant flowers. Listen to this, this is a spooky one:

> *Behold me here as you pass by:*
> *As you are now so once was I.*
> *As I am now so shall you be,*
> *Prepare for death and follow me."*

"That's more like it," I said with a little shudder. "More what you'd expect from a graveyard."

"That's Jeremiah Southwick," Lindy told me. "Died in 1862, in the middle of the Civil War. I've always wondered if that was the epitaph he wanted, or if somebody picked it for him after he was dead. He might be really ticked off, wherever he is."

I explored on hands and knees, discovering large upright plaques and tiny headstones nearly overgrown with weeds, some with deeply chiseled inscriptions and others with names and dates that were nearly obscured. There were sentimental epitaphs: "Taken from us, preserved for God!" and markers which told stories, such as four members of the McDowell family buried together in 1856, victims of some accident or epidemic. I imagined the voices of mourners breaking the quiet, where I crouched now among the fallen leaves and untended stones.

I felt deliciously free from observers. No one worried that I would fall and hurt myself, no one stared and marveled at how well I was getting around. If Lindy watched me at all, it was only to learn if I was as fascinated as she had hoped I would be.

"I'm getting hungry." Her voice shattered my solitude. "Let's have those sandwiches."

At first I felt a sense of sacrilege, sitting down to eat on a stone which read MADELINE GABRIELLA THORNE, but after the first bite I discovered how hungry I really was. Maybe Madeline would just be grateful for our company.

"There's a beautiful yellow butterfly!" Lindy exclaimed. "He's not even afraid of us, he just landed on a dandelion right behind you. . . . Now he's gone. Hey," she asked suddenly, "do you know what colors are?"

"Not really. I was born blind; I can't even imagine what seeing is like."

"Do you mind me asking you?"

"No, why should I mind?"

"Okay then—when I said just now there was a yellow butterfly, what did you picture?"

"A butterfly that was, oh, kind of glossy. I guess I translate colors into textures without even thinking about it. Like red would be hot, and gray would be kind of dusty, and brown would be soft like a dog's fur."

"How about pink?"

"Like a baby's skin."

"And green?"

"That's easy. Leaves and grass."

"There ought to be a way I could describe it." Lindy paused, thinking hard. "Like blue. Well, it's a soft color usually, but not always though—and if you mix it with yellow you get green. . . ."

"But I still don't know what blue is," I reminded her. It wasn't the first time someone had tried to unravel the mystery for me. "I don't think it's explainable. Like I couldn't explain what a violin sounds like to a deaf person."

"I'm going to think about it," Lindy promised. "Now I've gotten started—there must be some way."

I picked a few burrs off my socks. "Don't worry about it. I don't."

The sun's warmth had gradually faded, and I drew my jacket closer around me. "It's clouding up," Lindy said. "We better start home if we don't want to get caught in the rain."

We gathered our trash into a paper bag to carry it out with us. I took Lindy's arm and followed her back to the road.

"Now I know why you wouldn't tell me where we were going," I said.

"I was a little afraid you'd think it was weird or something." She kicked a pebble ahead of us.

"I would have, probably," I admitted. "But it's a neat place. Do you know of other places like that?"

"Lots!" Her voice shone with eagerness. "We can go to the marble quarry, and to this old empty house I know of, and there's a dirt road marked *private* I've never even explored."

For a fleeting moment I thought of Karen. Karen would tear her stockings on the underbrush, Karen would be afraid there might be snakes, Karen would have better things to do with her time than crawl around in the woods like a kid. Then, "Let's go there first," I said. "Let's check out the private road."

4

Miss Kellogg shut the book with a snap. It was one of those swift changes of mood that caught up the stragglers, pulled the wandering attention of the class back to the front of the room. I found myself leaning forward, eager for whatever was coming next.

"Meg, I'd like to read your composition aloud this afternoon. May I?"

A wave of heat swept up over my cheeks. "Oh no, please!" I burst out, sounding absurdly desperate even to my own ears. Somewhere in me there was a different response, a gracious "Of course, thank you" that never reached my lips.

Chairs creaked as people turned in their seats to look at me. I shouldn't have said anything. No one had ever before refused to have a composition read aloud. But I had never expected to share those thoughts with the inquisitive crowd around me; they had been intended only for Miss Kellogg.

"It's very well written," she said. "I think everyone will enjoy it." I wavered. "It's not always easy, listening to someone else read your work," she went on. "But it might be a good experience for you."

"Okay." My voice sounded flat and defeated. Part of me tingled with excitement and pride, but it wasn't betrayed by that thin little "okay." Tense on the edge of my chair, my hands interlaced on the nicked desk top, I waited for the ordeal to begin.

Miss Kellogg had asked us to write on the topic "How Nature Affects My Life." There had been the usual grumblings: "What kind of effects is she talking about? Like when it rains and the game gets called off?" Now, as Miss Kellogg's clipped New England accent read the words I had heard before only inside my own head, I remembered the hours I had spent at my desk, and the pages I had ripped from my Braille writer to crumple into balls for the wastebasket, before I was ready to type the final version.

"The floorboards in our attic are unpainted," she

began, "and in the summer heat, beads of sticky sap still ooze from tiny cracks, the blood of the trees that went into building our house."

The room was too still around me. I forced myself to lean against the back of my chair, to draw a long, quavering breath.

"The carpet beneath my feet is made of sheep's wool; the dress I am wearing is of cotton cloth; the metal in my typewriter was mined out of the earth. It is easy to forget that in one way or another all of the food we eat comes from animals and plants which were once alive. As we eat and breathe, we ourselves are part of the never-ending natural cycle.

"I think that we need to remember that we are part of nature, as much as the deer and the raccoon. When we pour detergent down our drains, when we throw away plastic bottles that will not decompose for thousands of years, when our cars exhale exhaust fumes into the atmosphere, we are not only making the world uninhabitable for wild creatures that are fun to watch but are somehow dispensable, we are gradually making the world uninhabitable for the human race as well."

Like some machine that I couldn't switch off, Miss Kellogg's voice swept on, revealing all. I wondered what Karen had written about. Somewhere behind me she was listening, wondering perhaps what I, a blind person, could know about such things, about anything.

"I can't think just in terms of the effects nature has on my life, because my life is inseparable from nature. I share the earth with the chickadees outside my window. But because I cannot help being part of what we call *civilization*, I cannot help contributing to the dangers that threaten the world."

The final words fell into the stillness, and then for a long moment of sustained agony the silence deepened around me. Then it shattered into little ripples of congratulation: "Hey, that was good!" "Wish I could write like that!" But I couldn't trust them—after all, what else could they say, embarrassed as they were into being polite?

Miss Kellogg walked to my desk and handed me the folded sheet. "An A," she whispered. Miss Kellogg liked it, and nothing else mattered quite as much as that. As I slipped the paper into the back of my notebook, the glow I felt was not embarrassment, but pride.

"I think Meg brings up some pretty interesting issues," Miss Kellogg was saying. "You know, I bet most of us go for days without ever stepping on a blade of grass. When I was thirteen I told everybody I was going to go live in a cabin like Thoreau. They all laughed and told me how cold and damp I'd be, and how the mosquitoes would eat me alive, and somehow I got the idea—you weren't supposed to rebel against the comforts of home."

She was off again on one of her tangents. The sighs and shufflings around me spoke of boredom and impatience, mingled with relief that we would surely not return to regular classwork today. With luck, she would even forget to assign homework.

Slowly my tense muscles relaxed, and I leaned back to let her ideas flow toward me. The theme was always the same, her outrage against the world that existed and her enthusiasm for what could be instead.

"The problem is, who's deciding for us what a home should be? G.E. tells us we need a new electric can opener, General Motors convinces us we can't be happy without a new car each year. And we take their word for it. What do you think would happen if someone campaigned on the platform that we dismantle Detroit and use bicycles and—sure, why not —horses? It could be done, parking garages could be converted into livery stables. I'm serious. But they'd fight it every inch of the way; they'd be afraid of losing money, losing control. And we go along with whatever they dictate, like sheep. . . ."

Two sharp buzzes from the telephone by the door severed the sentence. "You see? They heard me!" she said with a laugh as she crossed the room to answer it. She lifted the receiver with a faint click. "Hello? Yes. . . . Yes, she is. You want her right away? . . . All right, I'll tell her. Fine. 'Bye." The receiver clicked back into place.

"Meg, Mr. Wallace would like to see you."

A pang of fright shot through me. No one was eve[r] called to the principal's office unless there was som[e] kind of trouble. "Right now?" I asked, though I wa[s] already on my feet, gathering up my books.

"Right now," she answered.

I felt stiff and unreal, walking to the door past th[e] curious glances of the others. As I stepped into th[e] hall I heard Miss Kellogg resume: "It's always easi[er] to conform, just to go along . . ." before the closi[ng] door cut off her words.

Wildly I searched my memory for some infrin[ge]ment of the rules, but I could find nothing. Mr. W[al]lace liked me, I assured myself. Hadn't he given [me] a special hall pass? I hurried down the deserted co[rri]dor, sliding the tip of my cane ahead of me along [the] base of the wall. There had to be a simple expla[na]tion, and in a few minutes it would all make se[nse.] But the nagging certainty persisted—I was sure [that] no good could come of this, whatever it might be[.]

The clatter of typewriters and the smell of prin[ting] ink led me straight to the half-open door of the [main] office. I went in and rested my hands on the [glass] topped counter that ran almost the width of the [small] room, and waited for someone to notice me.

It was an endless wait. My nervousness yield[ed to] impatience as people came and went around [me] completing their transactions. "Mr. Wallace se[nt] me," I said at last to a rattling typewriter on my left.

"Right through there." The secretary's voice was heavy with annoyance, the kind of annoyance that is constant and has nothing to do with people or situations. "Go on! What are you standing there for?"

"I'm sorry—where is he—where should I . . . ?"

"Over there!" Then she must have spotted my cane, or read more closely the incomprehension on my face, for she scraped back her chair with an exasperated sigh. "Here, I'll take you."

Bony fingers dug into my arm above the elbow as she thrust me forward. "Watch out, watch out," she said after a few steps. She jerked to a stop and propelled me around the end of the counter.

"I'm okay," I tried to soothe her, but her anxiety seemed to increase with every step. We crossed two small rooms, bound together by my helplessness in the unfamiliar surroundings. My book bag bumped against a chair, and her grip tightened.

So I actually felt relieved when I found myself in a narrow doorway and heard my escort explain, "She says you sent for her."

"Oh, Meg! That didn't take long, did it?" The secretary released my arm, and quick footsteps carried her away. "Here, have a seat."

His voice was full of smiles. I took the hand he extended, and he showed me to a leather armchair where I sat, facing him across a glass-covered desk.

My exploring fingers found a staple gun, a beanbag ashtray, and a large roll of Scotch tape before I became self-conscious and folded my hands primly on my lap.

"Well, how've you been doing? I've been hearing some good reports."

"Oh, I'm doing okay, I guess." Already it was clear that he hadn't called me in for a reprimand. I allowed myself to relax.

"Listen, Meg, let me tell you why I wanted to see you." He leaned toward me. I caught again the smell of cigars and shaving lotion. "You know we've got our annual Parent-Teacher Night coming up next week. The parents have a chance to come visit the school and meet their children's teachers. I'm wondering if you'd be willing to help us out."

"Well, sure. Doing what?" I was completely drawn in by my desire to feel useful. I pictured myself handing out information sheets at the front door or, quietly competent, directing bewildered fathers and mothers down the right corridors.

"I'd like to see you set up a little exhibit of all your —uh—special equipment. Most of the parents and teachers would be pretty interested to see how you manage. You could be there with your Braille and all, answer questions . . ."

"No!" I cried. "I'd hate it! I'd hate them all coming to stare at me, like in a museum!" I forced myself to a stop and groped for reasons that he might accept.

"Oh no, certainly I never meant you to think of it like that. You'd just be at a table with your Braille and whatever other special equipment you use, just sitting there to answer questions."

"I don't have that much to show them. I just use a regular typewriter for my assignments and for tests in class . . ."

"But it has specially marked keys, doesn't it?"

"No, I touch type. You're not supposed to look at the keys anyway with touch typing."

"No, of course not. That makes sense. There, now you see, you've taught me something already. I think you have a lot to teach all of us."

"I don't want to do it," I repeated.

I heard a faint squeak as he tilted back in his swivel chair. "Look, this is nothing to feel embarrassed about. Everyone is very impressed with the things you've accomplished. You can't operate in some of the ways normal people do, but you've compensated beautifully. It's nothing to be ashamed of."

The bell rang. Mr. Wallace's office was insulated against the tumult that broke loose in the halls every forty-two minutes. "It might be a good experience for you," he went on, "and I know the parents and teachers would appreciate the opportunity . . ."

"I have to get to my next class," I told him, though it was only study hall. I stood up. "I'm sorry,

but I really can't do it. I'm not explaining it very well, I guess, but I just can't."

"I'm sorry you feel this way," Mr. Wallace said. I took his arm and followed him out the way I had come. "But think about it, and stop by in the next day or two if you change your mind."

"Okay," I promised, to appease him. "I will."

"I hope you will. Take it easy now." He patted my shoulder. " 'Bye."

" 'Bye," I echoed. Gratefully I stepped through the door to blend into the churning stream of humanity that poured through the halls at the bell's command.

5

"Well, did he?" I couldn't mistake Karen's voice, bubbling with giggles even when she was only talking to another girl. I stood motionless, straining for her words above the rush and gurgle of water.

"It's no big deal," the other girl answered. Someone ripped a paper towel from the dispenser. "He asked me, so I said I'd go. What are you doing?"

"I'm going with Jeffrey again, I guess. Oh phooey! Just look at this, will you? A big pimple on my chin— it wasn't there this morning! I'm supposed to go out tonight!"

My hands trembled a little as I swung open the door of the booth and stepped out. They continued their conversation as I made my way to the row of sinks.

"What's the matter with Jeffrey? I thought you dug him."

"Oh, he's okay." I was close enough to hear the comb crackling through Karen's hair. "I just don't want people to get the idea we're going steady or anything. I just want to have fun."

I pressed the lever, but no soap trickled onto my palm. Karen turned as I moved to another sink, and we nearly collided. For the first time she seemed to notice me.

"I'm sorry," she greeted me. "I didn't see you. There's a sink right here." She placed my hand on the porcelain rim. "The soap's up here—I'll get you some."

"I'm okay. I can do it," I said patiently. There were times when I grew tired of my old refrain, when I ached to slap the helping hands and to jeer at the solicitous phrases. I rubbed my hands in the stinging stream of hot water and waited for them to resume their talk, hoping that somehow I would be able to join in.

"Well, good night," said Karen's friend, as though my arrival had somehow cut off the flow of their conversation. "I'll call you tonight and tell you about it."

She was gone through the pneumatic *whish* of the door. Karen and I were alone.

I was alone with Karen, who asked Jeffrey to parties, who didn't want people to think that she and Jeffrey were going steady because that would interfere with "having fun." My jealousy pulsed into life. I wanted to assault her with questions: How could she treat a date with Jeffrey Allen, with *Jeffrey Allen*, like a punishment? What was the secret to her popularity? Was it the practiced perfection of her giggle, that bright bubble of laughter that always surfaced just at the proper moment?

But it was Karen who spoke first. "Meg, do you mind if I ask you a question?"

I suspected what kind of question she had ready, and toyed with the idea of replying that I did indeed mind. I braced myself and said, "No, go on."

"Ever since I met you, I've been wanting to ask . . ." She hesitated, torn between curiosity and embarrassment. With subtle malice I waited, letting her struggle. "I've been wanting to ask you—I keep on wondering—how do you get dressed in the morning?"

"I put my dress in the middle of the room, and then I swing out on this rope that hangs from the ceiling and jump into it feet first."

I forced a laugh out into the stunned silence. There was an answering chuckle, equally forced, from Karen.

"Hey, I didn't mean . . ." She trailed off, because of course she had meant.

"I'm sorry, I didn't mean to put you on the spot," I said, though I had richly enjoyed it.

I wiped my hands with studied concern and waited for the impasse to be broken. At last Karen could no longer stand the silence. "Well, how should I know how you do things when you can't see? I never met anybody before who was—like you."

Even then, I couldn't resist the urge to interrupt, "You mean you never met anybody before who was fifteen years old, and five feet four, and lived in Ridge View . . ."

"Okay, okay, so I'm dumb, all right?"

The upper hand was securely mine, and I could afford to be generous. "It's just that there's nothing to it," I explained. "I just get dressed and eat and everything the same way other people do, as far as I know." I found the wastebasket with my right foot and dropped in the crumpled paper towel. "If you closed your eyes you'd find out you could still do everything."

"I ought to try it sometime. But I'd probably trip over my own feet."

"I doubt it." I found the chair where I had piled my books and gathered them up.

"Here," Karen said, "let me get the door for you. Can I take you anywhere?"

"No, I'm okay," I said again.

"I don't learn too fast, do I?" Karen said. "Well, so long then."

" 'Bye," I answered. I turned and retreated down the corridor, not even sure where I would go.

It was only a quarter past three, but already the halls were nearly deserted. I walked aimlessly, made an unnecessary trip up to my locker, wandered through the school store and past the library, crushed by the enormity of my aloneness. I had never tried to share my deepest feelings with anyone, and much of the time had even masked them from myself—the pain of being observed, labeled, and excluded; my growing fear that I might never have a place in the thrillingly active, complex world of normal people. Mom and Dad looked for a trouble-free flow of pleasant events from day to day, and a hint that I was not happy would only be proof that things were not working out. Though Sam was easygoing and accepting, he was too young to be a true confidant. Lindy could rage with me against Mr. Wallace's stupidity, and we could share marvelous adventures, but she seemed totally satisfied with her role as eccentric. She would never understand my longing for dates and parties and all the other trappings of growing up.

It was true that I meant to find out if any offerings for the *Messenger* had been left in the box marked MANUSCRIPTS on Miss Kellogg's desk. I entered Room

68

Two Thirty-four as casually as if I had no other pur-
pose, as if I had not hoped to find her there alone.

"Hi, Meg." Her voice reached out to me from behind her desk. "I've been sitting here grading papers,
wondering why it's so quiet around here this afternoon."

I asked if any contributions had come in, and she
showed me a ragged stack of papers, bristling with
paper clips and wrinkled corners. Tomorrow, she suggested, we should begin to make our selection. If we
tried, we could have the *Messenger* out by Christmas.
That gave us more than six weeks. And could I talk
to Mr. Baranowski in the basement and find out if
he could print it on the offset press? A thousand
copies, fifty pages each. Yes, of course, I could handle
that. . . .

The meaningless words rattled around my ears
while my opportunity to speak slipped farther and
farther from me. I didn't know what I wanted to say;
I only felt the intense need to communicate, perhaps
to have my feelings verified or dispelled. At last my
pretext for being there was exhausted; we had completed all of the business at hand. Defeated, I turned
to go.

"Is something the matter, Meg? You look a little
pale."

Miss Kellogg's words drew me back. It was the
opening I had needed. "Do you know what happened

to me just now?" I exclaimed. "Karen Cardelli just asked me how I dress myself!" I rushed on, not giving her time to respond. "And Mr. Wallace wanted to put me on exhibit for Parent-Teacher Night next week! When I come into a room, people stop talking to look at me. I just want to go out and have fun like the other kids. I don't want to be some kind of weirdo!" My eyes stung with tears of self-pity.

Miss Kellogg walked around the desk and laid her hand on my shoulder. "It's hard—don't I know it!" she said. "You want so much to be part of the in crowd, but everything in you works against it. Chances are you wouldn't even enjoy the things they do, but you can't believe that now. . . ."

"I just want to be—to be . . ." I fumbled for the right words. "Normal. Not different, not strange. Maybe people just don't ever get used to someone who's blind, maybe it's just too big a difference."

"You think your being blind is the only difference between you and Karen Cardelli? You are different—that day in class Karen wanted to write that cummings poem off as nonsense, but you listened, you wanted to understand it, even though it was new to you. . . ."

"That doesn't help me get invited to parties!"

"Maybe not, but it's why you probably wouldn't like those parties if you were invited. As you get older, go to college, get out into the world, it should get easier to meet the kind of people you can really share things with. I hated high school myself. I felt like I didn't have a single friend there when I graduated. I was so down on school of any kind by then, I refused to go to college and ran away to live in Greenwich Village."

She paused, as though drifting back into her memory, and I sat down in one of the empty seats in the front row. Miss Kellogg took a seat across the aisle. "Where did you live before, when you were in high school?" I asked.

"Lynn, Massachusetts. They used to say, 'Lynn, Lynn, the city of sin, the more you do, the more you're in.' It's a mill town, not much there. I could have gone to Boston, but that felt too close to home. So I spent a couple of years in the Village, scribbling poetry and telling myself I was rebelling against all the world's evils. Finally I figured out that the world didn't care if I sat in my fifth-floor walk-up with my typewriter. I wasn't bothering anybody. So I went to college and became a teacher."

"To try and get through to kids somehow?"

"To try, at least." For a moment she fell silent. "I tried in Boston for a while, but that was too much for me. So last summer I moved down here. But I don't expect my story to make you feel any better. I suppose you can't learn from anybody else's experience. Sometimes you have to discover things for yourself. But if it's any help to you at all I'll remind you of what Thoreau said—I guess if I've ever had a hero in my life it's Thoreau—anyway, he said that each of us marches to the beat of a different drummer. Maybe you could say that growing up is really just listening for the right beat."

There was a step in the doorway. "Hi," said Keith Howard, shattering the mood of intimacy. "Am I interrupting something?"

"Come on in," Miss Kellogg said, and I wished him at the bottom of the ocean.

"I just came by to see if the *Messenger*'s gotten any submissions yet. Are these them? Wow! We've got a ton of reading to do."

"You both should come by tomorrow afternoon and start reading them over." Miss Kellogg rose and walked to the back of the room. Her coat rustled as she took it from the closet. "They'll be surprised when they see what kind of magazine we've put together. I've got a feeling they won't be any too pleased."

"Who won't?" Keith asked.

"Maybe I shouldn't be telling you this," she said, returning to the front of the room, "but certain people in the administration are pretty curious to know what I'm up to. Now let's see, have I got everything I need?"

I slipped into my coat and collected my belongings.

Keith and I followed Miss Kellogg to the door. She must have been pointing to the public-address system speaker in the corner when she said, almost to herself, "I've always wondered if they've rigged it to work the other way. We listen to them, but can they listen to us?"

A little shiver started between my shoulders and hovered for a moment in the middle of my back. Could Mr. Wallace be tuning in on us, tilted back in his swivel chair, wearing a set of earphones and switching from one classroom to another with the flick of a dial? The irritable secretary would be his partner, of course. . . . But there was a flaw somewhere. Mr. Wallace just wasn't smart enough to be a spy.

"Good night," said Miss Kellogg when we reached the office. "Teachers have to sign in and out every day. Makes it easier for them to keep track of me."

"What do you think?" Keith demanded as soon as we were alone. "Don't you think she worries too much about things sometimes?"

"About things?" I was guarded. "What do you mean?"

"You heard her. All this stuff about Mr. Wallace. It's kind of strange, isn't it?"

"Well, who knows? Maybe the rooms *are* bugged," I argued. "They can broadcast, who's to say they can't listen in?"

"But why would they?" Together we leaned against the front door. It creaked and swung outward. We stepped into the chill of the late afternoon.

Keith didn't ask me where I lived, or if I needed any help—he just walked me home. He did most of the talking—about the *Messenger*, about a play he had attended with his parents, about his dream of writing the libretto to a modern opera someday. "Hey," he said, when we reached the flagstone walk that led up to my front steps, "I've been meaning to bring you those records. The *Ring* cycle might be a little too heavy for you just at first, but maybe you'd like something more popular, like *Carmen* or *La Bohème*."

I hadn't exactly forgotten that he was the boy who sang opera on the street, but somehow I had managed to block the grim memory into a back corner of my mind. Now it burst back into my consciousness.

"Sure, that'd be nice," I said, but suddenly I wanted to get inside. "See you tomorrow. We can look at those manuscripts."

"Okay. I'll bring you *Carmen*. Some of it will be familiar. You've heard this, haven't you, the 'Toreador Song'?"

I listened in dismay as he hummed a few opening lines. At any moment he would burst into song!

"Yes, I think I have heard it before. So long, be seeing you."

"Okay, see you tomorrow." His voice lifted, filling out the melody, and swept away up the street.

Sam flung the door open before I put my key into the lock. "Meg's got a boyfriend!" he chanted. "Meg's got a boyfriend!"

I threw down my book bag and launched myself at him. His collar jerked from between my fingers, and his feet thudded up the carpeted stairs. "Meg's got a boyfriend! I saw Meg's boyfriend!" he sang over the banister as I reached the bottom step.

"I do not!" I shouted, my cheeks on fire. "Quit it!"

"For heaven's sake!" Mom emerged into the upstairs hallway. "Keep the noise down!"

"Mom, guess what!" Sam cried. "Meg's got a . . ."

But I had him, clapping one hand over his mouth while with the other I tried to pin his wriggling arms behind his back.

"Calm down!" Mom begged. "You're giving me a headache."

"Mom, make him quit pestering me!"

With a mighty wrench, Sam freed himself and scrambled to the safety of his room. "Mom, look! Look where your daughter scratched me! She ought to cut her nails!"

"All right, that's enough out of both of you," Mom asserted. "Samuel, I already asked you once to pick up your room. Meg, come downstairs and set the table before your father gets home."

"Meg's got a boyfriend," Sam taunted softly as I followed Mom downstairs.

"Brat!" I hissed back from the landing.

"What got all that started?" Mom asked.

"Oh, nothing. I just walked home with this boy I know from working on the magazine."

"What's he like? Is he nice?" Mom tried to sound nonchalant, but she couldn't conceal her curiosity.

"He's nice enough, I guess," was all I would tell her. Perhaps if I had walked home with Jeffrey, I would have been eager to take her into my confidence.

"You could have invited him in," she said wistfully.

"How could I invite anybody in with Sam around?" I muttered, and went to set the table.

I lay awake a long time that night listening to the familiar creakings of the house, the chime of the clock downstairs marking the quarter hour, now and then the distant blare of a car horn or the screech of brakes. I thought of Jeffrey, and tried to imagine how Karen could be so indifferent toward him. But thoughts of them only revived the pain of my isolation. No matter what Miss Kellogg said to console me, I longed to be part of their group. I would be forever relegated to live among the outsiders, people like Lindy and Keith and Miss Kellogg. As much as I liked her, I knew that Miss Kellogg was an outsider too.

She said so often enough, and it was true. My days in the Braille class had never been so crammed with questions and complications.

I must have dozed at last, for the sound jolted me upright, and I sat on the edge of the bed for a moment, dazed and uncomprehending. It drew nearer as my mind cleared, a medley of clean, mellow notes. I sprang to fling open the window and drink in the honking of the southbound Canada geese.

They were so close now that I could distinguish individual members of the flock, some voices high and clear, others deeper and more husky, discordant, yet blending like an orchestra tuning up. My nightgown fluttered in the breeze, but I didn't notice if it was cold. Leaning on the sill, I followed their course over the roof, out across the patch of woods behind the house. I clung to the last traces of their music, as the sigh of the wind in dry branches and the murmur of distant traffic rose to engulf it. I couldn't be certain when the last echoes had faded away. For a minute more I strained after them, until the cold crept over me and I slid the window shut.

I felt peaceful when I slipped back under the patchwork quilt, and I dropped at once into a restful, dreamless sleep.

6

"I saw a poster once that said THINGS ALWAYS TAKE LONGER THAN THEY DO," Lindy said as the afternoon drew to a close. We all laughed in appreciation. It was certainly true of the *Messenger*. The Christmas deadline had seemed reasonable enough, but already we had discovered that many of the stories submitted were of the "What I Did Last Summer" genre; the secretary in charge of supplies had refused Miss Kellogg's request for one hundred reams of top-grade paper; and Mr. Baranowski would not print the magazine without written authorization from Mr. Wallace. We would have to follow procedures, we were told. We must learn to go through the proper channels.

"Well, what did I tell you?" Miss Kellogg sounded almost triumphant. "I knew they'd put up obstacles. Someone mentioned today in the teachers' room that the twirlers and the cheerleaders are costing the school twelve hundred dollars this year for a set of new uniforms. But they can't afford two fifty for the paper we want." Her keys jingled as she locked the door behind us. "Can I give anybody a ride?" she asked.

As usual, the other members of the *Messenger* staff had trickled away one by one during the long session of reading and discussing. The three of us, Keith and Lindy and I, clustered in the hall, trying to read one another's responses to the amazing offer. Teachers didn't drive students home.

But Miss Kellogg did things that other teachers didn't do. Lindy explained that she had her bicycle, but Keith and I thanked her and followed her to the faculty parking lot.

"It's hardly worth it for me to go home," Miss Kellogg said, opening the door on the driver's side. "I've got to be back by seven for Parent-Teacher Night."

She reached across to open the door on the right, and Keith and I crowded into the front seat. "I'm really not supposed to be doing this," she confided.

"They say it's because of the insurance, but basically they think it's unprofessional." She turned the key in the ignition, and the motor purred into life. "Now, where do you need to go?"

It was all so mundane, this talk about where to make a right turn, and which streets were only one way, that the miracle was almost obscured: We were here with Miss Kellogg, away from the world of regulations which defined so rigidly the roles of teacher and pupil.

"You don't need to be in any hurry getting those records back," Keith said, turning to me. "You need to hear them a couple of times to get into them."

"What sort of records?" Miss Kellogg asked with interest.

"An opera, *Carmen*, he wants me to listen to," I explained, a little awkwardly. I didn't want Miss Kellogg to imagine, as Sam did, that Keith was my boyfriend.

"I'm always trying to convert people," Keith said. "It's kind of lonely when nobody else is into your kind of music."

"You know," Miss Kellogg said, "Ridge View is so close to New York, but people hardly ever go into the city to take advantage of the opera and the theaters and that sort of thing. Suburbia's so anesthetized by TV, nobody ever leaves their living rooms in the evenings."

"I went to the Met with my folks last year," Keith said. "I couldn't believe there were so many people in the world who'd pay to see *Rigoletto*."

"It's pretty expensive, isn't it?" I asked.

"They've got some cheaper seats in the top balcony," Keith said. "This season they're doing *La Traviata*. You can send for tickets—it's announced in the Sunday *Times*."

"We'll make it a cultural enrichment project," Miss Kellogg decided. "We'll get upper balcony seats, and go to celebrate the first issue of the *Messenger*."

"Oh, let's!" I cried, forgetting that I had ever dreaded Keith's singing. "Let's ask Lindy, too."

"I'll get the tickets," Keith was chattering. "They should be around five dollars, maybe a little more if it's a Friday or Saturday, but that's okay—even the seats there are nice, real cushiony with lots of room for your legs. You can get a pretty good view even from the top balcony, and you can hear fine from up there, that's the main thing."

"Of course, we'd better keep this to ourselves," Miss Kellogg warned. "They'd have some unkind things to say if they found out. It'd be just one more strike against me, fraternizing with my students. I'm subverting good TV-watching American youth."

"And guess what," Keith went on. "I read there's a chance Beverly Sills might sing Violetta!"

"Teachers have been fired for less in some schools,"

Miss Kellogg continued. "They're always looking for something . . ."

"Hey," Keith interrupted, "that's my house back there! I forgot to pay attention. You can let me out right here."

"We'll do it," Miss Kellogg said, pulling over to the side of the road. "I'll look forward to it."

"I'll write for the tickets tonight," Keith promised, opening the door. "Can you imagine hearing Sills live?"

"Are you sure we should go?" I asked, as we drove on. "I mean, if you might get in trouble . . ."

"Never mind them," she said. "I can't live my life trying to appease them, can I?" We rode in silence for a minute before she asked, "By the way, are your parents coming tonight?"

"I don't know." I thought of Mrs. Gomez. "Maybe they made some other plans. I didn't remind them. I guess in a way I don't want them to go."

"How come?"

"I've been having a lot of trouble with algebra, and if they talk to Mrs. Gomez they might make a real fuss." When I put it into words, it didn't seem quite as dreadful.

"I never liked math much either till I went to college," Miss Kellogg confessed. "Then I had a really wonderful professor, Dr. Albion. He kind of showed us the mystical elements of higher mathematics—

you're dealing with things like imaginary numbers, and formulas that can help you understand what matter is and how the universe works. At the very least it's a puzzle to work out, and when you really get into it it's kind of magic."

"I never thought of it that way," I said, but I was not ready to change my views.

"Now, which house did you say is yours?"

"Thirty-seven."

She slowed the car. "Thirty-one, thirty-five, thirty-seven. Here you are, right at the walk."

"Thanks for the ride," I said. I searched for the door handle, found it, and stepped out.

"I hope I get to meet your folks," she said. "I can't say I'm really looking forward to tonight myself."

"See you tomorrow," I called. The car gained speed and moved away up the street.

We were going to the opera, Lindy and Keith, Miss Kellogg and I. We were venturing together from Ridge View out into the real world.

My hope that Mom and Dad would be too busy, or that they would forget completely that tonight was Parent-Teacher Night, had never been very strong. It perished quietly at the dinner table when Mom remarked that now, finally, she would have a chance to talk to "that algebra teacher of yours."

"I don't know why anybody'd want to talk to Mrs.

Gomez if they could avoid it," I observed. My fork pursued a chunk of beef that skidded to the edge of my plate.

"If she's any kind of a decent teacher she'll want you to learn," Dad said from the head of the table. "Let's face it, Meg, that means giving you a little extra help."

"Listen, I spend forty-two minutes a day with that lady already. That's five days a week . . ." I attempted some quick mental calculations, but Sam was faster.

"That's two hundred and ten minutes a week," he announced. "That's three hours and forty minutes."

"And that's too much time already," I concluded. "The one you ought to meet is Miss Kellogg. She's in Room Two Thirty-four."

"We've heard so much about her, we wouldn't want to miss her," Mom said. But they hadn't forgotten the long hours I spent crouched over algebra homework, or the C minus Mrs. Gomez had awarded me on the first report card. I knew they would head for Mrs. Gomez's room as soon as they stepped through the double front doors.

"We just want to be sure that everything's working out," Dad said, to complete my thought.

From my desk after dinner I heard the front door slam, and the tapping of Mom's heels down the front walk. Downstairs Sam switched on the television, and the house was filled with the crash of rifles and the screams of terrified horses. Volume Two of my algebra book lay open before me. I ran an apathetic hand down the page and found the first of the problems Mrs. Gomez had assigned that morning.

"Mary's mother is four times as old as Mary is. Mary's cousin is ten years older than Mary and two-thirds the age of Mary's mother. How old is Mary's mother?"

I pushed back my chair and went to join Sam downstairs in the den.

He sat at the card table, which was strewn with tiny plastic cowboys and Indians, cavalry, and a pile of Lincoln Logs. I drew up a chair and began to sort out the Indians and their horses.

"What's this show about?" I asked when the commercial began.

"It's just over," Sam said. "I think there's a good movie coming on."

With a luxurious sigh, reveling in his freedom from parental surveillance, he rattled through the paper in search of the television listings. I was tempted to play the role of big sister by reminding him of his homework, but it was pleasant to be delinquent together.

"Wow! *Scaramouche* is on Channel Seven!" He bounded to the set and twirled past three stations to stop at the chosen one. "Man! This is a neat picture! He goes after this guy in a duel. . . ."

In the kitchen the phone rang.

I was sure it would be for Dad, some business acquaintance who must be treated with perfect courtesy. Still I made a wild dash and caught it on the third ring. In the fragment of silence following my "Hello," I imagined an answering "Hi" in Jeffrey's voice.

"Hello." It was a girl. I would not acknowledge that absurd prick of disappointment. "Is this Meg?"

I struggled toward recognition. It couldn't be . . .

"Karen?"

"Hey, you recognize my voice already. Listen, I want to ask you something. . . ."

This was the moment! Meg, I'm having some kids over on Saturday, could you . . . ?

". . . Have you got the homework assignment for Miss Kellogg's class tomorrow?"

I had no right to be disappointed. It was my own fault. I should never have expected anything else. "Sure. You've got to write about either the person who most influenced your life, or else man's responsibilities."

"Bum-mer!" It came out as a long sigh. "I guess I better figure out who influenced my life. I don't get what she wants in that responsibility one, do you?"

"I'm not sure." I had begun the composition, and the more I thought about it, the more complex the subject had become.

"I guess my mother influenced me. We don't always get along, but I guess I'll write about her. Who are you writing about?"

"I'm working on that other one," I admitted. "The one on man's responsibilities."

"Well, like what do you think about it? I just can't get into it at all."

I pulled up a chair from the kitchen table and sat down. In some way that I didn't fully understand, I knew I had something that Karen wanted. "Well, there's responsibility toward each other, toward the environment, toward ourselves."

"Wow! I bet you get an A," Karen said. "My Mom'd flip out if Kellogg ever gave me anything above a C. And you can't even— Oh, I'm sorry, I just meant—you know." She paused. "Meg, do you think you could do me a favor?"

"Sure."

"Maybe I can work on my composition for a while, and then call you back and read you what I've got so far, and maybe you could help me. I mean, just with some of the spelling I'm not sure of, and where to put the commas, stuff like that."

"I'd be glad to," I said, and fearing that I sounded too formal, added, "That'd be cool."

"Thanks a million. I'll call you back in an hour or so. Ciao!"

Slowly I lowered the dead receiver to the cradle. A strange new confidence surged through me. I still longed for Karen's normality, the key to acceptance by the group I wanted to be part of. But perhaps I had something Karen lacked. I had never before conceived that Karen might envy me anything.

I returned to my desk and once again read the problem about Mary's mother. If I let X represent Mary's age, and Y be her mother's age, then $4X$ should equal Y. I flipped back a few pages and read the example with all the steps worked out. I pounded out the opening steps on the Braille writer, my mind racing from one alternative to the next. It was almost fun, like a jigsaw puzzle once the first few pieces have snapped into place.

Four of the fourteen problems I had to leave unsolved, but I knew what questions I might try to ask in the next class. As I began to type out my answers to hand in to Mrs. Gomez, I realized that I had nearly enjoyed my algebra homework. Somehow it was because of Karen. Our conversation had infused me with new confidence, and I was spurred on to try harder than ever before.

A key turned in the front door. Mom and Dad were home from Parent-Teacher Night.

They came in exclaiming about the cold, and hung their coats in the hall closet as though they had been out on some ordinary excursion. I stood at the foot of the stairs, my nervous fingers tracing the roundness of the newel post, waiting.

"Sam, haven't you started your homework yet?" Mom's dismay rose above the jangle of a toothpaste commercial.

Dad's voice was stern in the sudden hush when the set was switched off. "What do you mean, you'll do it in the morning? You know the rule around here."

They emerged. Sam, subdued, passed me without a word. I followed Dad into the kitchen. "How did it go?" I asked, striving for nonchalance I did not feel.

"It was okay." He opened the refrigerator. "We finally got to talk to your math teacher anyway."

"What did she say?"

Mom came in and began to unload the dishwasher. "I think she's willing to give you some extra help," she said over the clatter of plates. "She was a little short with us at first, seemed to think we were asking her to give you a grade you didn't deserve or something."

"Now you see how she is!" I was triumphant. "She's so impatient, she's that way with everybody. She just keeps going when half the class is lost."

"Well," Dad said, "she did agree to talk to you tomorrow about tutorial sessions. She said it was up to you to ask for the help and prepare for the sessions—so I hope you'll cooperate."

"Oh Dad!" I groaned. "I don't want to have to ask her for anything!" But I knew that if I wanted things to work out, I would go to Mrs. Gomez tomorrow.

Somehow the prospect was not quite as appalling as it might have been. Maybe Miss Kellogg was right. Maybe math could mean more than just random numbers on a page.

"What did you think of Miss Kellogg?" I asked.

"Oh, your English teacher?" Dad tore open a loaf of bread. "She seems interesting."

"She's certainly an unusual person," Mom said carefully. "She had a big spot right on the front of her blouse—she must have had time to go home and change it, but I don't think she even noticed. Maybe she was a little nervous."

"I'd be nervous too, if I had that mob waiting for me," Dad said. "There was a woman ahead of us in line complaining that her son says Miss Kellogg is—a little unbalanced."

A chill slithered down my back. "There must have been some parents who didn't feel that way," I protested. "There are lots of kids who like her."

"She certainly seemed glad to see us," Mom said. "She looked like she was going through quite an ordeal. But she had lots of nice things to say about you, Meg. She's very pleased with your work, says students like you make teaching worthwhile."

My delight must have shown on my face.

"She seems like an interesting person," Dad repeated, as though Miss Kellogg had somehow left him nothing else to grasp. "Very piercing blue eyes."

The phone rang. In two steps I crossed to the wall where it hung, forcing my whirling thoughts into order. I needed to have my mind clear to talk to Karen. Later, when I was alone, I would have time to ponder the things Mom and Dad had told me.

7

The fly buzzed in another circle around my head and drifted to the windows. The rattle of the rain against the glass would have lulled me into pleasant dreaminess if I had not been so acutely aware of Mrs. Gomez's lowering presence. Alone with her for the first time, I jumped whenever she opened a drawer or turned a page. She would be correcting papers at her desk, she told me, and I should interrupt her whenever I had a question. But I felt as though she was intent on every move I made, resentful of my intrusion, convinced that I would never learn anything.

My hair hung straight and lifeless, and the pages of my algebra book were limp with the dampness that pervaded the room. The desk was too small for my Braille writer, my typewriter, and my book. I arranged Volume Three, loosely bound between two floppy cardboard covers, on my lap. But the struggle against gravity made it doubly hard to concentrate on the first problem.

I read it again, the dots almost meaningless beneath my fingers. I reread the opening steps of the solution from the sheet of paper rolled into the Braille writer. Last night at home I had worked out a problem almost like this one, but now I felt comprehension slipping away from me again.

"How far have you gotten?" Mrs. Gomez advanced to my side and hovered over me ominously.

"Not very." I attempted a little laugh. "I guess I'm stuck."

There was no mistaking that exasperated sigh. I read aloud the two meager lines of Braille.

"You're right so far," she said. "Why did you stop there?"

"I don't know. I just can't figure out what to do next."

"Try multiplying by Y squared." She stepped back, but she was still watching me. For a long second, then another, I sat immobile under her scrutiny. "Space is a problem for you, isn't it?" she said at last.

"Well, kind of." My left hand held the book, still refusing to let it slide off my knees.

"Would it help if we brought another desk over next to you?" she asked.

"Hey, that might do it." Already she had taken hold of a desk in the next row and was pushing it across the aisle. I rose and seized the edge nearest me, bringing the two desks together. In the moment we faced each other, sharing the task, I sensed a warmth in her which I hadn't suspected. She was human, after all.

"I'll be here at my desk. We'll go over the answers whenever you're ready." And she was the old Mrs. Gomez again.

I spread Volume Three open on the desk beside me and read the problem again. The rain pummeled the windowpanes.

Every Monday afternoon between three and four—tutorial sessions with Mrs. Gomez stretched ahead like an endless series of appointments with the dentist. If I hadn't been blind, I might have been permitted to fail algebra in peace. I was surrounded by people who flunked tests, couldn't finish homework assignments, and made ridiculous mistakes in class. If I had been like the others, my achievements and defeats would not have been followed with such concern by everyone from my parents to Mr. Wallace. I couldn't do poorly in algebra without proving to everyone that "it didn't work out."

I multiplied by Y squared. The wall clock ticked once, like the slow turning of a page, to mark the passing of one more minute.

"We'll have to stop for today." Mrs. Gomez rustled into her raincoat.

"Thank you," I said, more grateful for my release than for the help I had received. I squeezed Volume Three into my book bag and bade her good night. I would not have to endure another special algebra session for an entire week.

I reveled in the stillness of the four-o'clock corridor. The silence reverberated with the delicate echoes set off by the walls and ceiling, so clear that I perceived the open door of a locker and swerved around it without breaking stride. Filled with the glorious sense of freedom from observers, I did not bother to unfold my cane. As I passed the study hall, deserted and locked for the night, I began to sing, "Are you going to Scarborough Fair . . ."

I had heard no telltale footsteps, and Karen's greeting caught me completely by surprise as I crossed the foyer. "Meg! What are you doing here so late?"

I bit off the opening notes of the second stanza and tried to hide my embarrassment. Keith wouldn't have been embarrassed, I thought fleetingly, before I answered, "I had to see Mrs. Gomez. How come you're still here?"

"Cheering practice. And then I had to hang around looking through the lost and found for my sweater, so everybody went on ahead."

She pushed open the front door, and the sound of the rain swelled louder. I hesitated in the doorway, fastening the top button of my raincoat and wishing I had brought a hat.

On the steps ahead of me Karen snapped open an umbrella. "Man, we need an ark for this one," she called. "Haven't you got something for your head?"

"No."

"You're going to drown. You better share my umbrella with me."

"Hey, thanks." My right hand seized the curved handle. Rain drummed inches above my head.

"Which way you going?" she asked.

"Up the hill, over to Prospect. Is that out of your way?"

"It is, kind of. I'm supposed to meet some kids down at the Burger Shop." I waited, breathless, while she struggled with the problem. "I suppose you could come with me, and afterward I could walk you home. Would you mind?"

"No, of course not." I fought my delight down to reasonable dimensions. "Let's go."

I had been to the Burger Shop before, after church on Sundays, or on hot summer evenings when Mom didn't feel like cooking. Always I had felt conspicuous, cloistered in a booth with Mom and Dad and Sam, while all around us boys and girls my own age laughed and flirted and played songs on the jukebox. It was not a place to go with your family. It was a place to go with your crowd.

Karen hardly stopped talking during the three-block walk into the center of town. "I never walked before with somebody that couldn't see," she began. "Just tell me if I walk too fast. My grandmother, she's blind, but she's not like you. She stays home mostly. But you know what? She likes to watch TV—well, she listens to it, right? She never misses *Love of Life*. Do you ever listen to TV?"

"Sure. Hey, did you see that special last night on UFO's? It was really . . ."

"You do? You do everything! Hey, what do you think I look like?"

"Let's see, you're about my height . . ."

"What color hair have I got?"

"Blond?" I hazarded. Her name was Cardelli, but somehow she had to be a blonde.

"You're amazing! How did you know?" Our little circle of shelter pressed on through the downpour.

Again I tried to shift the subject. "How was cheering practice?"

"Okay. We're working out the routines for the Thanksgiving game. Do you ever go to football games? I guess you might not enjoy them too much."

"I go sometimes."

"Someone could tell you what was happening, couldn't they. And you could listen to the cheering."

"Right," I said wearily. "I listen to the cheering." A passing car spattered my legs with mud. It had been a mistake to come with Karen. Umbrella or no umbrella, I would turn around and go home. "Listen," I began, "I just remembered something. . . ."

"Wow! I thought we'd never get here!" Karen folded the umbrella, cautioning, "Watch out, there's a little step—I've got the door," and with my will suspended I followed her inside.

I felt as though I had slammed into a solid wall of sound. The jukebox blared. A pounding bass and a melody that shrieked above it blotted out every trace of reality except the floor under my feet and Karen's arm, which led me away from any hope of escape. There were no voices around us, no echoes from solid walls or moving figures, only the throbbing of the bass and the jarring, exhilarated cries of the singer.

I felt Karen stoop; I touched the vinyl seat back and slid into the booth beside her. The others were there ahead of us. My toe brushed a stranger's foot under the table, and Karen was shouting to someone. I strained for her words and caught ". . . drowned rats! Did you guys order?"

I stripped off my wet raincoat and arranged it behind me. The music began its fade-out, and slowly the

room took form around me: the sizzle and clatter of
the kitchen off to my right, the sudden roar of traffic
as someone opened the door, and two girls talking
across the table from me. I prayed that no one would
feed the jukebox any more quarters for a while.

"Meg didn't have an umbrella, so she came with
me to share mine," Karen explained. "Meg, this is
Stephanie across from you, and this goof next to her is
Betsy."

There were two feeble hellos from across the table,
and I forced out a friendly hi.

Conversation gained momentum slowly at first, and
I feared that my unexpected arrival had thrown everyone into confusion. The waiter came for our orders.
Stephanie bemoaned the weather, and Betsy lamented
over her French homework. Huddled against my coat,
I searched for something to say that might put them
more at ease. But I was stricken with the shyness of a
stranger among close friends, afraid that my attempt
to enter their talk would be rejected or, even worse,
ignored.

The waiter returned. He strewed jingling knives and
forks over the table and set down his load of plates.
A warm, fragrant cloud rose from the dish he placed
in front of me. In a nest of French fries, I discovered
my hamburger in its plump bun, bristling with pickles,
lettuce, and tomato.

"Want catsup?" Karen asked.

Automatically I reached for the bottle, but my hand stopped in midair. Pouring catsup was a risky business, not to be undertaken under their scrutiny. "No thanks," I said, and bit into the dry chunk of meat in its dry roll. "I like it better plain."

Food had a dramatic effect upon us all. As we relaxed over sodas, hamburgers, French fries, and cole slaw, talk somehow began to flow more freely.

"Has anybody seen Joyce Giordano lately?" Betsy asked. No one had. "So nobody knows what color her hair is!" A little giggle played around her words, tickling our curiosity.

"It was black last time I saw her," Stephanie said.

Betsy assured us that it was black no more, and begged us to guess.

"Blond?" Karen asked.

"No."

Stephanie guessed, "Red?"

"Closer."

"Orange?"

"Green?"

"Blue!" I cried, as hilarity mounted. "Purple! Pink!"

"Pink! Who said pink?" Betsy demanded. "You all ought to see her! She dyed it for a costume party, and now they can't get it out!"

"Joyce is such a scream," Stephanie said as our laughter began to fade. "You know what she told me once? She said she was afraid to go swimming after the boys had been in the pool because you can get pregnant that way."

And when the laughter began to subside, Betsy set it off again by asking, "Well, do you blame her?"

I had hardly spoken, but the laughter engulfed all of us. I forgot about feeling unwelcome and found that I was having fun. They had been friends for a long time, and I was not one of them yet, but I was learning some of the rules. Keep the ball in the air, never let the mood drop. I listened to their banter in fascination, waiting for a chance to contribute some witticism of my own.

Betsy confided that she thought the waiter was cute, and Stephanie offered to pass the message along to him. Betsy shrieked, but already Karen was calling him over to our booth. Through the confusion of squeals and giggles he was finally told to bring Karen another root beer. He departed, leaving a wake of excited whispers.

"Hey, who's that?" Karen asked suddenly. "That lady that just got up, in the blue dress. For a second I thought it was Miss Kellogg."

"Lord help us!" Betsy groaned, and Stephanie made a gagging sound and said, "I'm going to lose my lunch!"

"It's not her," Karen assured them. "Look, this lady's hair is combed."

"Did anybody notice what she had on today?" Betsy

asked. "It was an okay dress for once, but the hem was hanging in front, and she had one sleeve turned up and the other one down."

"I was too busy noticing the homework she gave us," Karen grumbled. "First she told us to read three chapters in *Huckleberry Finn* and then she got off on prejudice for twenty minutes and forgot the first assignment, and wound up saying we had to write a sonnet."

"My mother gave her an earful on Parent-Teacher Night," Betsy said. "Told her if she didn't shape up she'd go to Mr. Wallace."

"Some of the stuff she says, about how we've got to watch out for mind control and all that, it's really nuts," Karen said. "She's getting to be a what-do-you-call-it, a paranoid."

"It's not that," I protested, "it's just that she believes . . ."

"She likes you," Karen said, as though it were an accusation. "And anyway, you don't have to look at her."

I crunched the last charred French fries on my plate in silence. I must not defend Miss Kellogg too eagerly if I wanted to strengthen my new foothold in the world of the normal and successful. I was still an outsider, but I was sitting where I had longed to be, with a bunch of friends at the Burger Shop. I wasn't really betraying Miss Kellogg, I told myself. I wasn't really going along with the crowd. I was just keeping my thoughts to myself.

"Well, Karen," Betsy said after an unexpected pause, "we're all waiting for the news."

"What are you talking about?"

"You know." The giggle crept back into Betsy's voice. "The big scoop."

"We saw you," Stephanie put in, "coming out of the cafeteria with him. . . ."

No, I decided, Karen probably didn't blush the way I would have in her place.

"Are you back together or what?" Betsy demanded. Something fluttered in my chest, but I sipped the last of my cherry Coke, waiting.

Karen sighed. "He snuck up behind me and put his hands around my neck, okay? When I screamed he still wasn't satisfied, had to follow me all the way up to Two Eleven."

"Well, you didn't look too put-upon when we saw you," Betsy asserted.

"Why should you anyway, walking around with Jeffrey Allen?" Stephanie voiced the thought that was churning in my own mind. I was suffused with my old jealousy, and with the recognition that I was still very far from being one of them after all.

"He's okay," said Karen. "He can be such a pest though, I mean it! Like sneaking up on me—you'd think he was ten years old."

103

"My father says when boys tease you it's because they like you," I said.

"Hear that?" chortled Stephanie. "Meg says he likes you."

"I just want him to leave me alone," Karen insisted. "I just want to have fun, go out with some other guys once in a while."

"But how can you feel that way when he likes you?" I really wanted to know. It was something I couldn't fathom.

But Karen wouldn't explain. "Let's get the check," she said, pulling on her coat. There were a few amplified clicks, and a drum thumped out the lead-in to another song on the jukebox. It was time to go.

The rain had stopped, and I drew deep lungfuls of the sweet, cleansed air. It was good to be outside again.

"Thanks for letting me share your umbrella," I told Karen. "I can make it home from here myself." We faced each other for a moment, and I realized that I didn't really dislike her. It was only that she made me long for things I didn't have, but perhaps, after all, they weren't beyond my reach. "I had a good time," I concluded.

"Good. Maybe we'll do it again sometime."

I didn't really like the commotion of the Burger Shop, the repartee sometimes left me far behind, but I would learn. If I had made mistakes today, I'd have a chance to do better the next time. Karen had said I might join them again.

But on my walk home I found myself looking forward to Saturday. Lindy and I were going to hike out to the old marble quarry, and a hike with Lindy was always an adventure.

8

One day after school during the first week in December, Miss Kellogg led Keith, Lindy, and me to the supply closet at the back of her room and revealed the hundred reams of top-grade paper which the supply secretary had refused to purchase for us three weeks before. Suddenly the Christmas issue of the *Messenger* was a reality again.

"But how?" I demanded, as she tore open one of the blocklike packages.

"Suffice it to say that there are ways and means." Miss Kellogg handed me a sheet of paper, thick, smooth, and costly, exactly what the *Messenger* deserved.

For the quality of the content was going to match the quality of the paper. For more than a month we had solicited contributions. Slowly and patiently, the others taking turns reading aloud, we had sifted through stacks of manuscripts and made our final selection: seven short stories, four poems, and an essay about ecology. On Miss Kellogg's urging, one of the poems, "From the Far North," about migrating geese, was mine.

We spent forty-five minutes planning the final layout, and at last Miss Kellogg locked the manuscripts into her drawer and went for her coat. It was time to go.

"I've got news!" Keith announced. "We've got balcony seats for *La Traviata* on Friday the nineteenth!"

I had felt especially close to the three of them that afternoon, as we shared our enthusiasm for the embryonic *Messenger*, and I knew that I would love nothing more than to spend an evening with them away from school, discovering the marvels of New York. I couldn't imagine how Keith had guarded his secret all day, saving it until we were all together and had completed the business of the afternoon.

"The *Messenger* will be out that week," Lindy said. "It'll be a celebration."

Through our excited chatter I heard Miss Kellogg

lock the supply closet and erase the blackboard. We drifted toward the door, calculating how much we owed Keith for the tickets. I picked up my book bag and took Lindy's arm.

"Good night!" Miss Kellogg called, too loudly to be addressing us. "We're leaving now, you can switch your earphones off! Hope we didn't bore you!"

She clicked off the lights and we stepped out into the hall, too stunned to speak. We should have had a hearty laugh over the picture of Mr. Wallace surrounded by listening devices, but there was something about the way she spoke that left me with a knot at the pit of my stomach. Instead of reassuring us, she went on in a low voice, "They're dying to know what I've been doing during all these late meetings. They've been watching me pretty closely the past week or two."

She stopped at the office to sign out, and we went on down the hall without her. "She's going a little overboard with some of this stuff about being spied on, don't you think?" Keith said.

"I keep hearing some of the other kids say she's going around the bend," Lindy said. "When she comes out with something like that, I start thinking maybe they've got a point."

"But you know what Wallace is like!" I argued. "He probably can't stand her doing anything that's different."

"You've got to admit, though," Lindy said, "something very strange is happening to Miss Kellogg."

But I had to admit nothing of the kind. "You know how much homework Gomez gave us tonight?" I demanded. "Twenty-three problems! She called on four kids in a row this morning that had the wrong answer, so that's how she's getting back at us!" And as I drew their attention to the gross injustice of it all, I didn't have to think that anything very strange was happening to Miss Kellogg.

In the days that followed, I had to try harder than ever not to listen to disturbing scraps of conversation. A boy in homeroom complained that Miss Kellogg had lost his composition, and that she had excused herself by claiming that someone had been taking things from her drawers. Two girls ahead of me on the lunch line guffawed while a boy exclaimed, "*They* are everywhere! Watch out! *They* will make you into robots!" On the way into assembly one morning a girl whispered, "Make way for Crazy Kellogg!"

As though she sensed the growing hostility, Miss Kellogg's references became more and more frequent. *They* were everywhere, listening, watching, suppressing free speech, enforcing the conformity which kept them in power.

But through it all, she went on teaching us about literature. She filled the bookshelves with contributions from her personal library and encouraged, almost begged, us to borrow and read. She departed from the English department's standard anthology and had us read *The Catcher in the Rye* and *Brave New World*. She opened each class with a quotation from Emerson or Thoreau or some of her other favorite thinkers: "Whoso would be a man must be a nonconformist"; "A foolish consistency is the hobgoblin of little minds." There were days when even Karen became drawn into the discussions that ensued.

But all the while there was grumbling. Miss Kellogg had such weird ideas, people said. We hadn't worked on grammar in weeks, and how were we going to pass the standardized final exam? What right did Miss Kellogg have to look down on people just because they didn't worship her lousy books? Some of them were even pornographic—and what would Mr. Wallace say if he found out?

"What'll happen if a whole bunch of kids get their parents to complain?" I asked Lindy one day on our way up from the cafeteria.

"I don't know," she said, "but we ought to be finding out pretty soon."

There was a different feeling in Miss Kellogg's classroom that day. There was more than the usual stirring and shuffling as she read us a short passage from *Civil Disobedience*. She tried to prod the class into a discussion, but there was mutiny in the insolent popping of gum and rustling of pages. Lindy brought up the modern war resisters. I related the readings to the sit-ins of the civil rights movement, trying desperately to keep the discussion alive. A girl named Andrea who always got A's threw in Mahatma Gandhi.

There was a gaping pause.

"Yes, Bill," Miss Kellogg said. I thought I detected a shaky note somewhere in her voice.

"If you were going to civilly disobey," said Bill from the row by the windows, "wouldn't *they* do something to stop you?"

At the back of the room, someone cracked his knuckles.

"Of course," Miss Kellogg replied. "The powers that be will always try to stop protests—it stands to reason . . ."

"*They* wouldn't want you to speak your mind, right?" interrupted the gruff-voiced boy named Warren two seats behind me. "*They* might throw you in jail if you disagreed with them."

A titter ran through the room, but still Miss Kellogg tried to hold her ground. "People are being jailed for resistance today," she said. "It's dangerous to take a stand. . . ."

"Especially with *them* watching and listening all the time!" It was Harry Wilson, his voice openly taunting. "I'm scared to say a word just thinking about it."

"*They* could be listening right now," Bill said. "Maybe we better check outside the door."

I wanted to spring from my seat, to shout them into silence, to make them leave her alone. But the sense of my own helplessness overwhelmed me. This was an organized conspiracy. If I stood against it I would only become another victim, or be ignored completely. So I listened, outraged and powerless, as the drama unfolded.

Now the room clamored with jeers and raucous laughter. There must have been others besides Lindy and myself who refused to join in the heckling, but our silence did nothing to counteract it. The voices merged into one hoot of mockery after another.

Then Miss Kellogg's voice cut through it all, shaking with fury. "Stop it, all of you! Sit down! *Shut up!*"

The room never quite returned to order, but slowly the ringleaders seemed to lose their control, and Miss Kellogg made herself heard. "I'm ashamed of all of you," she said. "You have a lot of growing up yet to do." After a moment's pause, she added, "Get out your grammar books. Turn to Chapter Three."

It was unnatural to hear Miss Kellogg at the front of the room, outlining subject and predicate with squeaky chalk, announcing that we should expect a quiz on Friday. At last the clock gave a single tick, and there was a rustle of books and papers as we gathered our things together, anticipating the bell. I shut my grammar book and wedged it into my book bag. For the first time all semester, I couldn't wait for Miss Kellogg's class to be over.

"That's right, get ready!" she cried. She snapped the stick of chalk and flung it to ping against the wastebasket. "Be machines, if that's all you want out of life! In thirty-five seconds, fifteen hundred of you will rise at the sound of a bell! Get ready—on your mark—get set—*go!*"

The bell rang right on cue. In unison we rose and stampeded from the room.

"What's going to happen?" Lindy demanded as the stream of traffic swept us through the corridor. "Things can't go on like this—she's breaking!"

A smell like rotten eggs caught my nostrils as we passed the chemistry laboratory. "I don't know," I said, my mind numb. "I just don't know."

I sat through two more classes before the dismissal bell at three o'clock, but I didn't hear a word. What distressed me even more than the class's treatment of Miss Kellogg was the way I had slipped into helplessness. Perhaps she thought I condoned the others simply by refusing to oppose them. I had been one of the first to pack up before the bell rang, and I had fled from the room with the rest. I hadn't wanted to be there any longer. Something in Miss Kellogg's voice, in the snap of the chalk, frightened me.

Warren and Bill and the others had established

their own kind of law, and no one had dared to disobey. At three o'clock I made my way back to Room Two Thirty-four.

Miss Kellogg was there alone, rifling through papers at her desk. Not even Lindy had come back to see her. I felt a glow of self-righteousness as I approached her across the empty room.

"Hello, Meg. What can I do for you?" She sounded strangely distant, abstracted. The self-righteous glow faded. I took a step back.

"I just wanted to tell you—to tell you how sorry I am about this afternoon." My words dropped uselessly into the space between us.

For a long moment, Miss Kellogg didn't answer, and I began to wonder if she had heard me at all. When she did speak at last, I could still not be certain that she was addressing me. "They'll see," she said quietly. "They think they've got me cornered." Her pencil scratched on the desk blotter. "It isn't teaching, just to follow their lesson plans, just to pump in the information that'll be on their standardized test." Her voice rose. "I only want to teach, but they're afraid to let me!"

She paused, and I said, "You've taught me a lot, Miss Kellogg. I never knew there were so many things to read. . . ."

But she went on as though I hadn't spoken. "They've been going through my desk at night, looking for evidence." She pulled open a drawer and rummaged through its contents. "I code my notes now—I wish I could show you, Meg—my planbook, my notes on the students, they can find them, but they won't be able to read them."

"But they won't search your drawers, will they?"

"You'll learn." She slammed the drawer shut. "You're just too young to believe it yet." She lowered her voice to a whisper, and I leaned forward to catch her words. "They want me out of here. I can tell. It isn't the first time."

"Not everyone!" I found myself whispering too. "There are lots of us—me and Lindy and Keith and— lots of kids. . . ."

She stood up and scraped the chair into place un- under the desk. "They drove me out last time," she said. "They won't do that again. I won't give them the satisfaction. I'd rather quit first."

"But you can show them what you can do," I said. It was surprising how easily *them* slipped into my own vocabulary. "Wait till they see the *Messenger*. It's going to be good this year!"

"You're going to remind Mr. Baranowski about the printing, aren't you?" Suddenly she was almost the old Miss Kellogg again. The change was almost more frightening than the past few minutes had been.

"Sure," I said. "I'll talk to him tomorrow morning." She went to the closet for her coat. "Good night," I said. I didn't wait to walk out with her as I had on so many other afternoons. I heard her answer, "Good night, Meg," as I hurried out into the hall.

As I rounded the corner to pass the study hall, I heard Karen's unmistakable giggle ahead of me, and Stephanie gasped through her laughter, "What a trip! We laughed so hard Joyce almost wet her pants!"

"Hey," I called, hurrying to join them, "I haven't seen you guys around for a while."

"Hi, Meg," Karen said as I fell into step beside them. More than ever before I needed their laughter, their normality. "So he's coming," she went on, picking up some earlier thread of conversation, "and Rick, he's always a stitch; and Tony and Warren, and— who else—I can't even remember, I asked so many people—hey, Meg, you want to come to a party?"

"Sure," I said. It was all so easy, her invitation, my acceptance, that it didn't quite feel real.

"It's at my house on the nineteenth. That's a week from Friday. Can you come?"

"Sure," I repeated, "sounds like fun."

We passed through the front door out onto the sidewalk. The late-afternoon sun warmed my face despite the chill in the air. "I'll tell you more of the details next week," Karen said. "Ciao!"

It was not until their voices had nearly faded up the street that memory jolted me like an electric shock. *La Traviata* was on Friday the nineteenth!

It was too much to sort out after the muddled events of the afternoon. I walked home slowly, trying to absorb everything that had happened, struggling to come to the right decision. But when I was roused back to the world by boys' shouts and the bounce of a ball on the sidewalk in front of our house, I was no nearer a resolution.

Sam tossed me a quick hi and turned his attention back to the game. The date sang in my head as I climbed to the front porch and hunted in my pockets for the key. Friday the nineteenth! Friday the nineteenth!

9

On Wednesday morning, Karen called to me as I opened my locker before homeroom period. "I'm putting up posters for the Christmas Cotillion," she said. "Glad I ran into you. Listen, the party's at my house at eight. That's 17 Willow Court. It's kind of far. You live on Prospect, right?"

"Right."

"Well, Stephanie lives over that way. She can pick you up to walk over. You don't need to bring anything, we've got food and all that."

She tore off a long strip of Scotch tape. "Could you

hold this for me? Right here—like this." I held the poster steady, pleased to be even this close to the Christmas Cotillion.

"What should I wear?" I asked.

"Anything you want." She fastened down the last corner and stepped back to admire her work. "I've just got one more. Think I'll hang it over by the boys' gym. See you Friday."

"At eight," I said. I had made up my mind at last.

At lunch on Thursday Lindy and I laid claim to half of a table at the far end of the cafeteria, sharing it with two disdainful upper-class girls. Keith shouted to us over the din, and was already talking as we made room for his tray. "Mr. Baranowski won't print the *Messenger* for us next week! He says he's got programs for the choir concert, and some newsletter that goes out to the parents, and he says it's our own fault for not planning better."

"But he promised!" I protested. "He promised me just last week!"

Keith unwrapped what smelled like a tuna sandwich. "That was last week. This morning he said he thought we were only doing about three hundred copies, twenty pages each. He said he didn't know Mr. Wallace got us such good paper. He said even the newsletter's printed cheaper than that."

"So when will he print it for us?" I asked.

"Next year." For half a second he succeeded in catching us off guard. Then we all laughed with relief.

"Something's funny about all this." Lindy had been oddly quiet, and now, when she spoke at last, her seriousness was unnerving. "Where do you think Miss Kellogg got all that paper from?"

"What are you getting at?" I demanded.

"Oh, it's just a feeling." She crumpled a paper bag. "I've just got a feeling she's going to get into trouble over it. The way she's so mysterious, I think she didn't follow the rules somehow."

"Miss Kellogg's been acting real funny lately." I wondered why Keith insisted on stating the obvious. "Yesterday she told me again not to mention to anybody about the Met. Oh I know, she could get into trouble and all that, but it was the way she said it. She said it was just the kind of thing they were looking for, that by now they'd grab any excuse."

"To get rid of her." I completed the thought and we sat in silence. A few tables away someone dropped a plate, and a wave of whistles and applause swept the cafeteria.

"It'll be great to get away from here tomorrow," Lindy said. "This place makes me sick."

"Maybe Miss Kellogg'll feel better away from school," I said. "Maybe she won't feel so much like people are watching her when we're in the city." I felt as if I had never made other plans for tomorrow night. I wanted only to go with them to *La Traviata*. It was important for us to be together. I would simply explain to Karen that I couldn't make it to her party after all.

On Friday morning, Jeffrey was almost late to Mrs. Keene's history class. He thumped his books down on the desk seconds before the bell rang, muttering, "Man, she's really weirded out today!"

"Kellogg?" Warren asked across the aisle.

"You should have heard her this morning first period," Jeffrey said as the class grew gradually quiet. "She found out I was in favor of putting money toward a new trophy case for the foyer, as Class Treasurer, you know—and she said I was a *philistine!*"

I couldn't catch what Warren said—Mrs. Keene was pleading for order by that time—but Jeffrey's response was a rasping whisper: "I'm one of *them!*"

So, as I had suspected, Jeffrey too did not like Miss Kellogg. If he had been in our sixth-period class, he might even have been a leader in last week's conspiracy. I wished that life were less complicated, that all of the people I cared for would respect and appreciate one another. But all through Mrs. Keene's spiritless reading from last night's assigned chapter, I never thought of changing my mind about the opera. After class I would tell Karen that I was sorry, but something had come up, a problem at home—but maybe some other time . . .

In due time the bell rang again. I rose with the others and waited by my desk, listening for Karen's voice. Behind me Jeffrey said, "You're going to the party tonight, aren't you?"

I was so certain that he was speaking to someone else—to Warren, to anyone but me—that I didn't even turn until he said, more insistently, "Meg, I hear you're coming to Karen's tonight!"

Somewhere through the pounding in my ears I heard a thin voice answer, "Oh, are you going too? Guess I'll see you there."

I don't remember how my feet carried me down the hall, down the stairs, to the cafeteria. Suddenly I heard Lindy's greeting, we swept through the door into pandemonium, and I was shouting, "I won't be able to go tonight! My grandmother's real sick!"

The wind chased me all the way home. It tore at the scarf I had wound around my head, lashed at my face, disguised the sounds of traffic at the street crossings.

"I'm going to a party tonight!" I announced when Mom met me at the front door. "I've got to get ready."

In the warmth of the vestibule I stripped off my coat and scarf. My fingers felt numb and brittle, though I had worn woollen mittens.

"I thought you were going into the city tonight with Miss Kellogg." Mom handed me a wire hanger.

"That got called off," I said. "I can't figure out what to wear."

"Let's look through your closet," Mom said eagerly. She followed me upstairs, and we spent a long time sorting through my wardrobe, narrowing the choices down. Mom voted for my knit suit, but I said I didn't want to feel too dressed up—I was going to a party, not to church. I tried to imagine what Karen would be wearing—probably something sexy. Nothing like that hung in my closet. Mom still helped me shop, and for the first time I regretted that her taste governed my wardrobe.

At last we compromised on a dress with a deep V neck, puffed sleeves, and a long, full skirt. I had worn it only once before, and it hardly needed to be pressed. I felt elegant and graceful, the way it swished and floated around my legs when I paraded up and down the hall for Mom's inspection. It was just the sort of dress I could have worn to *La Traviata*.

I ran water into the bathtub, and Mom went downstairs to set up the ironing board. Through the closed bathroom door I heard her call, "Sam, we're eating early tonight! Your sister's going to a party!" Perhaps this was the first time all semester that Mom really believed things were working out for me. Perhaps even for her, my success at school depended on more than passing algebra.

Sam tapped my shoulder as I sat under the hair dryer, a book spread open on the table before me. I switched off the motor to catch his words, and they rang out in the sudden silence. "You got a date with your boyfriend?"

"Maybe." I turned the dryer on again.

"You gonna kiss him?" he shouted in my ear. "You gonna play spin the bottle?"

"Quit it!" I shouted back. "I'm going to a party, okay?"

The words danced through my head as I brushed out my hair, soft and shiny and still warm from the dryer. I bounded upstairs to slip into my dress. I'm going to a party, I'm going to a party!

Mom knocked and came in to help me with the finishing touches. She smoothed my skirt and fastened a silver chain gently around my neck. My appearance must be flawless. Nothing must mar the perfection of the evening.

Mirrors don't lie, but I could never be quite sure when people were telling the truth. Nevertheless, I asked, "Do I look okay?"

"You look lovely!" Mom said, and I could feel how much she meant it.

I rubbed a few drops of cologne behind my ears. I cleaned my fingernails again. I opened my box of earrings and decided not to wear any. I could think of nothing else to do, and it was only seven-thirty.

I was a grown-up, descending the stairs on high heels in a swirl of skirts and an aura of perfume. I knew that I was pretty. I was ready for the evening to work its magic, ready to meet Jeffrey in his own world.

I wandered into the den, aimless with waiting. From where he sat at the table, Sam gave a long wolf whistle. "Se-e-exy!" he drawled.

The television was on, but he was engrossed in a game at the table. I sat down opposite him and discovered the cowboys and Indians.

"I'm building the stockade over here," Sam said. It was a low open structure of wooden blocks with an entrance on one side and lookout towers at each corner. "These guys are on watch, but they're drunk, so they don't see the Sioux scouts. Hey, you can be the Sioux, and I'll be the cowboys, okay?" He handed me two tiny crouching figures with feathers sprouting from their heads.

We divided the men to form our respective forces. In addition to a collection of braves, I found that I had three papoose-toting squaws, a few barebacked horses, and a small plastic tepee. I set up camp before my scouts advanced on the unwary stockade.

Sam snored noisily. I rushed the scouts back to camp and delivered the news: "Paleface sleep! Too much firewater!" The braves did a brief war dance; I pounded out the rhythm of tomtoms on the flimsy table until the men jumped and tumbled, and Sam protested that I would make the stockade collapse.

But what would Jeffrey and Karen say if they could see me now, playing children's games? I was grown-up. I was going to a party. I would have to put an end to playing with toys and tramping through the woods. It was time for me to cultivate the feminine graces—dancing, an interest in clothes, skill in talking to boys.

The snoring broke off. One of the guards roused and called a slurred alarm.

I could allow myself this last time, knowing that it was the last. I could make a ritual of this end to childhood. I had this last battle—and the Sioux fought with a vengeance.

The stockade was in flames, the towers crashing, and Sam was protesting, "No fair, I shot that guy in the head!" when the doorbell rang.

10

Within a block of the house, I knew that Stephanie and I had nothing to say to each other. I asked her if she had been to parties at Karen's before; she answered that she had. I asked her who else was coming; she recited a long list of names, some of which were unfamiliar to me. After an agonizing silence, she asked me how many brothers and sisters I had. I regretted agreeing to let Stephanie pick me up. Even arriving at Karen's door chauffeured by Mom or Dad would have been better than this.

Karen's mother didn't come to the door until

Stephanie rang the bell a second time. We stepped from the cold into what felt like a wide, high-ceilinged room, smelling faintly of mothballs. My feet sank into a thick pile carpet.

"The kids are downstairs in the rumpus room," Mrs. Cardelli told us. "They're all throwing their coats in on Karen's bed."

Wordlessly Stephanie took my coat from me and disappeared across the carpet to some remote part of the house. Through the floor I could feel the steady throb of rock music.

"You can probably track them down just by following the noise," Karen's mother said beside me. "Karen says to me this afternoon, 'Mom,' she says, 'wait till you meet Meg! She can do anything!'"

"Oh, not really," I stammered.

Stephanie returned and took my arm. "Through here, right?" she asked. We left the carpet and crossed the linoleum of the kitchen, the music growing louder. Behind us Mrs. Cardelli exclaimed, "Watch the stairs, watch it, watch it," until her voice was drowned by the opening of the basement door.

Stephanie led me through the fog of noise to a sofa, and I sat down. Behind me was a wood-paneled wall; on my left I found a metal table with a glass ashtray and a few magazines. Voices milled around me and I could catch a few fragments of talk, but I could find

no point of entry. I waited alone on the sofa for something to happen.

The springs sank as someone sat down beside me.
Jeffrey had noticed my dress, my hair, the new look on
my face. . . . "Hi!" Karen shouted. "Want some
chips?"

I scooped a handful of potato chips from the
wooden bowl she held toward me. At least eating gave
me something to do.

"You want something to drink?" she asked.

"Sure. What've you got?" I shouted back.

"Coke, Sprite, beer . . ."

"Beer!" I repeated, startled. Hastily I tried to cover
my naiveté. "Your mother doesn't mind?"

"What she doesn't know won't hurt her."

"But aren't you afraid she'll come down here
and . . ."

"She wouldn't dare," Karen said airily. "So what do
you want? You want a beer?"

I had tasted beer before; Dad had sometimes made
a point of offering it to me while he watched a game
on TV, or when he came in after working in the yard.
I had never liked the taste much, and I would have
preferred a Coke, but there was no point explaining
that to Karen. "Sure," I said. "That sounds good."

The record was scratching endlessly in the last
groove, and no one bothered to change it. Off to my

left a boy called "Break!" and I heard the rapid clatter of pool balls. There were a few thumps as some of them dropped into the pockets. A little cluster of girls hovered in front of me. One of them said, "Well, if you won't, then I'll have to . . ." Her words were lost to the squeals of the others. Karen returned with my beer.

For a moment I held the tall, slightly sticky glass; then, gingerly, my lips touched the mound of foam at the top. I took a sip, and then another. It wasn't as bad as I had remembered.

"Karen! Challenge you to a game of pool!" a boy called. Karen drifted away, promising to be back in a few minutes, and again I was alone on the sofa. If I was going to enjoy this party, I would have to get up and mix.

I took another swallow of beer, counted to three, and stood up.

No one seemed to notice me as I advanced on a chattering group in the middle of the room. To wild whoops of laughter, Betsy was reminiscing about some past party she had attended, and how someone named Rick had gotten so "wasted" that he had rolled himself up in a throw rug and fallen asleep on the floor. Everyone else seemed to have a piece to add to the story—how Rick had stumbled around in the morning searching for one of his shoes, how he had managed to sneak into the house and convince his parents that he had been there all night.

I took another swallow of beer and found myself wondering if *La Traviata* had started yet. They would have climbed flight after flight to the top balcony, and now they must be perched high above the stage, studying their programs and thrilling with anticipation as the orchestra tuned up.

"Hey, let's have some sound!" I recognized Warren, one of the leaders in harassing Miss Kellogg. Jeffrey must not be here yet. I was so attuned to the sound of his voice that I would surely have discovered his whereabouts by now. Suppose he never came at all!

I couldn't allow myself to think about that. Jeffrey would come, and he would not find me huddled forlornly on the sofa, or mutely clinging to the fringe of the group. I would be flourishing in the thick of the action.

I had to begin somewhere. I would have to talk to someone.

"Put on the Dead!" Betsy was saying. "I want to hear the Grateful Dead!"

Someone obliged her, and the music rolled out to engulf us all. As though the music gave me courage, I heard myself saying to anyone who might respond, "That kid Rick, I don't think I know him. Is he here tonight?"

"Rick miss a party?" Betsy exclaimed. "You really don't know him! Sure he's here, over there at the pool table playing with Karen. That red-haired guy."

She didn't bother to correct herself, and I felt a gleam of triumph. At least my blindness was not the foremost thing on her mind. She had actually forgotten!

"Doesn't Karen's mother ever come down?" I asked.

"She'd be scared to death," Warren said. "She's probably upstairs right now drowning her sorrows." I didn't like the way he laughed.

"Where do you think Jeffrey is?" Stephanie asked behind me. I hoped I didn't change color when my heart lurched.

"I don't know, but he better get his body over here," Warren said. "He said he'd bring some weed."

The room was already heavy with smoke, and for a moment I was puzzled. Then, slowly, I began to understand—he wasn't referring to tobacco.

But before I had time to decide how I felt, Karen was asking, "Meg, do you know how to play pool?"

"No," I said, "I never tried it."

"You could do it, I bet," Karen said. "I'll show you."

"Okay," I said. I took her arm and followed her, a few potato chips crunching underfoot. She took my nearly empty glass and handed me a cue stick. I slid it between my hands, noting its gradual taper, the way it balanced when I held it at the thicker end.

"Now hold it like this," Karen said, showing me, "up a little—aim straight ahead of you and you'll hit the balls."

This was how Jeffrey would see me when he came in, wielding a cue stick, smiling and relaxed at the center of everything. I drew back my arm and thrust the stick straight forward. It grazed something solid, but nothing happened.

"A little lower," Stephanie suggested.

I took more careful aim and made another stab at the cluster of balls. This time I heard them chink together, and one bounced against the rim of the table. But the tip of the stick gouged into the felt, and I recoiled in dismay.

"Don't worry," Karen said. "The table's a mess already."

"Show her!" Warren urged. "Guide her hand!" Suddenly I was aware that a crowd had gathered around me. My confidence drained away. I shoved too quickly, almost dropped the stick, and again felt a sickening jolt as the tip dug into the felt. I didn't want to try again, but someone was readjusting my grip, readying me for still another effort.

It was then that Karen cried, "Finally! It's about time! Here's Jeffrey!"

I never knew if he had seen me at the pool table or not. The moment he was announced, the crowd around me disbanded and surged toward the foot of the stairs. "Hey!" Jeffrey called. "I hear there's a party going on down here!"

Everyone talked at once, and as the excitement swelled I was glad to be there. "Jeffrey," I cried into the confusion, sure that he wouldn't hear me, "we were afraid you weren't coming."

It was easy enough to find him—I just followed the crowd. "I could sure use a beer," he said, right in front of me. Bending toward him I heard the snap of a flip-top can, and his sigh of satisfaction after the first long gulp.

"Okay, you bring the stuff?" Warren asked. Again I felt a twinge of uneasiness. Maybe Jeffrey would say he was sorry, he hadn't had a chance to get it, and I wouldn't have to deal with grass tonight. Too many other things were going on; I had too much at stake already.

"Don't get greedy," Jeffrey said. "All in good time."

"Let's see." A plastic bag crackled, and Warren uttered an appreciative whistle.

Karen touched my arm. "Want another beer?" she asked.

"Sure. Thanks."

"Meg, I never knew you drank beer," Jeffrey said as Karen wandered off to refill my glass.

"I didn't know it either." Too late I saw that I had not made the proper comeback. I could have giggled provocatively and said, "There are lots of things you don't know about me." I could have said something that would make him look at me a second time, that would require an answer.

But already his attention had been diverted by Betsy, who offered him pretzels and bubbled her admiration of his shirt. "It's so groovy!" she exclaimed. "The colors are really psychedelic!"

I had nothing to say about his shirt, or about anything else that might interest him. When Karen returned with my brimming glass, I drew her into a discussion of the Grateful Dead. We drifted back toward the pool table, and I could no longer hear what Jeffrey and Betsy were saying to each other. I tried to tell myself that I didn't care.

After a while I found myself on the sofa again, this time between Karen and Warren. I only half listened to Warren's detailed account of a stock-car race. I had to admit that the talk bored me. The pounding music, the thick smoke, and the two beers had given me a headache. I was glad for the chance to sit still, not to seek anyone's approval.

I flipped open the lid of my Braille watch. It was almost ten o'clock. Maybe right now it was intermission at the Met. They would be stretching their legs in the lobby, exchanging comments about the performance. Keith would be ecstatic after listening to Beverly Sills for two hours and knowing that there was still more to come.

"You all right, Meg?" Karen leaned toward me.

"I'm okay."

"You sure? You look kind of down."

"Oh, I'm just thinking."

"Hey, don't get heavy!" she protested. "This is a party, remember?"

Someone cut the Grateful Dead off in the middle of a song, and replaced them with something lower and gentler by the Beatles. A sweet, pungent odor pricked my nostrils. Karen called, "Light the incense, will you?"

I shrank back against the sofa cushions. I wasn't ready to experience some strange new sensation tonight, to lose my bearings and feel more vulnerable than ever. Tonight I needed to keep my wits about me. Still, I listened in fascination as the ceremony proceeded, as Rick found and lit the sandalwood incense, as someone switched off the lights and replaced them with candles. Voices hushed. They had all gone through these motions before. This ritual had long been established to create the desired mood. But no matter how curious I felt, no matter how they urged me, I would say no. I couldn't take the risk here, couldn't plunge into the unknown with these strangers all around me.

"Want a hit?" Warren was trying to press something into my fingers.

"No thanks."

"Oh, come on! It won't hurt you!"

"I know—I just don't feel like it tonight," I said, hoping vainly to imply that I was as experienced as the rest of them.

"Don't bug her if she doesn't want any," said Karen. I smiled my gratitude as she reached across me toward Warren.

"Come on, Meg!" Jeffrey exclaimed. "It isn't any worse than drinking beer!"

A hot wave of anger swept me. "Okay, if it's that important!" I cried, startling myself with my own outburst. I snatched the thin roll of paper from Warren. My hand shook as I lifted the cold end toward my lips. They were all watching me. Was this some test, some rite of initiation that would determine my acceptance into the group?

"Hold it in and count to five," Jeffrey said with authority.

I took a long, defiant pull, dragging the smoke into my lungs. It clawed at my throat while I waited for my mind to be mysteriously transformed. Then my lungs exploded into a paroxysm of coughing that flung me against the back of the sofa, where I leaned, gasping for good, clean air.

"You're not used to it," Karen said when I caught

my breath. She handed me a glass and I sipped her beer. "It'll get easier."

"It doesn't seem like much fun to me." I could breathe again, but there was still a bitter taste in my mouth.

"Oh, you don't know what you're missing," Jeffrey said.

I do too know, I wanted to tell him. On account of you I'm missing *La Traviata*.

I was an outsider, I thought, as their laughter and meaningless words fluttered around me. Why had I ever imagined that I could be anything else? Perhaps even if I could see, I wouldn't fit into a gathering like this. But I had dreamed for so long of finding a place among normal people that I felt suddenly empty. There was nothing I really wanted. I was completely alone.

I had rejected my only real friends, and they could never forgive me when they found out. To Miss Kellogg I would be just another mindless conformist. Keith and Lindy could never understand my betrayal. But Karen's circle would never admit me either, and besides, I was beginning to realize that I would never really be happy there.

"Come on! Why's everybody sitting around?" Karen demanded. "Let's dance!"

Again the music was a meter of the party's mood. Now it became loud and pulsing, and in a moment I sat alone on the sofa. Soon it would be ten-thirty, late enough for me to plead tiredness and go home. But I didn't move, locked in my place by the misery of my loneliness. Feet stamped on the cement floor, and I caught fragments of talk as the dancers swayed and circled past me. "I'm starving!" Betsy said. "Let's send out for . . ." Then Jeffrey was in front of me with an unknown partner. "Dad's on the Town Council . . . got to listen . . . paranoid . . . !"

"Rollin', rollin', rollin' on the river!" Even in my despair I found my feet tapping to the electric rhythm. What must it be like to dance out there, to share that exhilaration with a partner? It wouldn't have to be Jeffrey—Rick, Warren, anyone would be all right. Longing swelled inside me so that I was tempted to join the dance alone, to step out and seek a partner since no one sought me.

I half rose from the sofa, but my legs buckled beneath me. An invisible wall separated me from the dance floor. I could not join them. I would go home. But I sat still while the music wound down to its final gasp. For one instant the room hung suspended in silence. Then Karen uttered a long, satisfied "Wow!"

"Wow!" the others echoed. They were panting for breath. The sofa sagged as people dropped down on either side of me.

"Blow out the candles," Jeffrey said. "Let's play the flashlight game."

There was a chorus of assent, followed by shrieks of excitement as they plunged into darkness. Now was my chance to escape. I rose and moved carefully along the sofa, stepping over protruding feet. I skirted some wooden chairs and headed for the stairway. No one would miss me. There was no point in saying good-bye.

"Hey, get Meg to hold the flashlight!" Warren cried.

I froze. "Meg, where are you?" Karen called. "We're all equal now, we can't see either!"

I didn't have to answer. I could still sneak away. But curiosity held me back. Maybe I had misjudged everything after all. They hadn't forgotten me. What was this game that they wanted me to share?

"I'm right here."

Karen found me, her groping hand brushing across my face. "Boy, Meg, I don't know how you do it! Here's the game. We all dance in the dark, see, and somebody holds the flashlight and shines it around the room, and whenever it shines on a couple, just by chance, you know, they've got to kiss. Okay?" She pressed the flashlight into my hand.

It all made sense. Too astounded to think, I said, "Okay." I found the switch and felt the glass warm faintly as the light came on. Maybe this was what I deserved for deserting Keith and Lindy and Miss Kellogg. What had I expected, anyway? I sat on the sofa and waited for the music to begin. "After a while somebody else can take a turn," Karen promised, but I didn't believe her.

To wild screams of laughter, I played the beam back and forth before me. When the shrieks intensified I held the beam steady for a few moments, trying to imagine what it must be like out there, dancing, being close, being kissed. "Hey Jeffrey, Jeffrey and Betsy, you're supposed to stop when you're in the dark!" Warren protested, and there was a loud guffaw.

I threw the light in a long arc that must have taken in everyone by the time it ended. Then I switched the flashlight off, laid it on the sofa, and stood up.

"Hey, what are you doing?" Stephanie wailed.

"I'm going upstairs to the bathroom," I announced. I didn't care who heard me.

"Get my mother to show you where it is," Karen said. As I searched for the stairway she went on, "Joyce, you take the flashlight for a little while, all right?"

I paused at the first doorway I found. It was not the stairway. I heard a rustle of clothing and a girl's giggle. A boy's voice demanded, "Who's that?" I stepped back and slid my hand farther along the paneled wall until I found the stair door and then the end of the banister.

In the kitchen beside the humming refrigerator I took a few deep breaths and felt the smoke clear out of my head. Behind me the music still pounded through the closed door, and I could still hear an occasional shout of laughter.

A television was on somewhere, a little too loud, and I followed the singing and applause down a carpeted hallway, past a stand of plastic flowers, to find Karen's mother. She spotted me in the doorway and hurried toward me, chattering, "You need some help, dear? Didn't my daughter even have the good manners to show you upstairs?" Her voice was too loud, too, and her breath reeked of alcohol.

"May I use your phone?" I asked, stepping back a little.

"Sure. It's in the kitchen." I followed her back the way I had come. My long dress dragged around my ankles. Behind us a voice intoned, "And now, a very important message!"

"What's the number?" she asked. "I'll dial it for you."

"I can do it." But she watched me as I counted the holes, and stood by to listen. "Hi, Mom, can you come pick me up? I'm at 17 Willow Court."

"Come sit with me," Mrs. Cardelli said when I put down the receiver. "You can keep me company."

She showed me to an overstuffed chair in the television room, where a little boy was boasting that he had no cavities. "You like the party?"

"It was all right."

"Listen, don't give me the gory details, okay? Kids

are kids and all that. They've got to have their fun. I just don't want to hear about it. I don't want to get old before my time."

I didn't know what to say. I hoped she would stop talking when the commercial was over, but when the host returned with his mystery guest, she went on, "You know, my daughter admires you so much. She tells me how smart you are, and talented—wish some of it'd rub off on that kid of mine! If her father'd drop by once in a while maybe he could do something with her. But she tells me you walk to school and dress yourself and everything."

Just call me Supergirl, I wanted to tell her. I could do everything but be asked to dance. I could do everything but kiss a boy.

"I hope you're not offended," she went on, "but, well, my mother doesn't see either. So I've learned how to help a blind person. When we go out to eat I always cut up her meat for her."

Mrs. Cardelli explained how her mother listened to soap operas, and how you could almost forget that she couldn't see, and how Karen better not try to get married before she turned eighteen. I was glad that she wasn't my mother. The host was winding up his interview with the promising young starlet when the doorbell rang.

"Listen, just promise me one thing," Mrs. Cardelli begged as I jumped up. "Just don't go complaining about anything to your parents. I don't want them calling me up to give me any grief, okay?"

"Okay," I promised. She found my coat on Karen's bed and shepherded me to the front door.

"We thought you'd be later," Dad said from the driver's seat. "We weren't going to worry till midnight."

Beside him, Mom asked, "How was it?"

"Oh, not a big deal." I lapsed into silence in the back seat.

They must have guessed that something was wrong, but still I knew that I shocked them when I announced, "I think I'd like to go to the Institute next semester after all."

11

"Let's talk about this." Dad shut off the motor in the garage, but no one moved to get out of the car. "What's on your mind?"

"Nothing." My movements felt smooth and slow; I reached for the handle, opened the door, stepped out. I walked up the driveway and turned onto the slate path to the back door. Behind me Mom and Dad talked in low voices. I waited for them inside the kitchen, my mind blank.

"Tell us what happened at that party," Mom pleaded.

"Nothing happened. I just changed my mind about school, that's all." I drew off my coat and started for the hall closet. There was nothing to say.

"Come sit in the living room for a few minutes," Dad urged. Reluctantly I followed them to sit in the easy chair beside the cold fireplace. Only a few months ago, sitting in this same chair, I had declared my intention to attend public school. Now I sat alone, even with Mom and Dad on the sofa across the room, even with the creak of the stairs as Sam tiptoed down to listen.

"We thought things were going so well," Mom said. "You were keeping your grades up, you seemed to be making friends . . ."

My voice was flat as I broke in. "It isn't working out."

I had nothing more to tell them. An enormous tiredness crept over my body and mind. I needed the solitude of my room, away from their questions, away from the worried, mystified glances that must be passing between them.

At last Dad said, "We don't want to push you, Meg. Let's sleep on it. We can talk about it some more in the morning."

"Of course it's up to you," Mom said. "But it'd be a shame to give up now. We've been so proud of you."

At the top of the stairs I felt Sam's shy touch on my

arm. "Good night," he said. For a moment we faced each other, waiting to say more. "Good night," I answered, and shut my door behind me.

My room was a safe place. I walked around it slowly, touching familiar objects—the polished conch shell on my bookcase, the peacock feather that arched above the bureau, the egg-shaped stone weighing down loose papers on my desk. There was comfort in the rapid ticking of my alarm clock and the rattle of the windows in the wind.

I was not going to cry. In defiance I kicked off my shoes, bracing myself against the tears that churned inside me. I draped my party dress, limp and lifeless, over a chair, and sank onto the bed. I was not going to cry. I was going to think.

I would never belong to Karen's crowd. I would never walk proudly down the halls of Ridge View High with Jeffrey Allen, envied by the girls, gaining new respect from the boys. I had always believed that I would become a different person if I could travel with the popular crowd, no longer the blind girl—peculiar, pathetic, or awe-inspiring—but a girl to be seen with, to flirt with, to introduce to friends. Now I knew that I didn't enjoy Karen's parties, and I didn't even like Jeffrey very much.

I should have felt relief. It had been exhausting, the struggle to conceal my differentness, to do and say the right things at all times. I should have been able to go back to Lindy and Keith and Miss Kellogg, to value their uniqueness, to nourish my own.

I flung myself full length on the bed, stifling my sobs in the pillow. I had treated them terribly. They had been my friends, and I had been ashamed of them. If they had never guessed it before, they had to know it now. I had not gone with them to the opera. I had lied and gone to Karen's party.

After a while my sobs turned into shivering. I crawled beneath the bedclothes, drawing my knees up to my chest, trying to bring warmth back to my trembling body. I was tired and disappointed, but at least I had made a decision.

I would finish out the semester at Ridge View. Then, in little more than a month, I would enter the Institute for the Blind, a world apart, where I would be just like everybody else.

As I floated into sleep I heard the howling of the gale around the windows, and somewhere a loose awning banged steadily against the house.

I woke with the sun's warmth sifting between the curtains onto my face. It was Saturday. I stretched luxuriously beneath the patchwork quilt, free from the hurry of weekday mornings.

Then the memory of last night jolted me wide awake. I burrowed deeper under the blankets. If only I didn't have to remember, or think, or look ahead!

"Meg, Sam—aren't you kids going to have any breakfast?" Mom called from the foot of the stairs. There was no use trying to hide. Slowly I got up, put on my bathrobe and slippers, and padded downstairs.

The smell of fresh coffee mingled richly with the aroma of cinnamon rolls warming in the oven. "Looks like we may be in for some snow," Dad said from behind the paper.

At any moment the questions would begin, and I would have to explain everything. Mom and Dad would only worry more if I continued to be evasive. But I had tried for so long to protect them from anxiety about me that now I didn't know how to talk about things that went wrong.

"This cold front's from the Great Lakes," Dad went on. "They got six inches in Buffalo last night."

"Don't forget to take your vitamin this morning." Mom slid the bottle of tablets toward me. "Yesterday you dashed off without it, didn't you?"

I poured a pill onto my palm and gulped it dutifully with my orange juice. How could I tell them about the way I had treated Lindy and Keith and Miss Kellogg, about Karen and Jeffrey and the party, about the exhausting, fruitless struggle to be like the others? They were proud of me. They thought I was doing well, and they didn't want to hear anything else. They hadn't mentioned the Institute in weeks.

Sam's bare feet thumped across the linoleum.

"Don't you own a pair of slippers?" Dad inquired. Sounding half asleep, Sam muttered that he couldn't find them.

It must be almost as hard for them to ask as it was for me to explain, I realized. I poured a bowl of cereal, waiting for the question that had to come.

It was Mom who spoke at last. "Well, Meg," she said, "have you thought any more about the things we were discussing last night?"

I set down my spoon and took a deep breath. "I've been thinking about them. I guess I've pretty much made up my mind." I waited for her to demand why, but when she said nothing I had to continue, "I guess maybe I'll like it better at the Institute after all. I won't feel all the time like the only one that's weird."

Sam banged his glass down on the table. "Cop-out!" he exclaimed. "There are lots of kids in that school weirder than you!"

"Sam," Dad broke in, "leave your sister alone. She's talking about a very serious decision."

"She's copping out, if you ask me," Sam said.

"Well, nobody did ask you!" I shouted. "You wouldn't like it either! You'd have quit a long time ago if you had to have everybody staring at you like you were some kind of freak! Don't think you're such a big shot!"

"That's enough out of both of you," Mom said. "Let's be reasonable about this."

"He isn't being fair!" I was almost ready to cry. Sam was making it all so much harder than it needed to be. "Make him keep out of it! It's none of his business!"

"You're really sure this is what you want?" Dad asked.

"I'm sure." The words were easy to say. It was settled. I would not try to take the words back. "I'll finish the semester," I said. "I can start in February."

"It makes sense," Dad said. "You've been under tremendous pressure. I think you're making the right choice."

The telephone rang, two long, jarring rings, before anyone moved. Then Sam and I sprang for it at the same moment, and he got there first. I waited, unwilling to sit down and resume the conversation. "Hello," Sam said. "Yeah, she's here. You want to talk to *her*?"

My heart was already pounding when he thrust the receiver into my hand, and something tightened in my throat when I heard Lindy's voice in my ear. "Hi Meg. Listen, how's your grandmother?"

I swayed on my feet. She knew, but she was trying to trap me in my lie. I swallowed hard, but before I could find an answer she was saying, "I was afraid to call you, in case this might be a bad day for your family or something. Is she . . ."

"Oh, she's okay, she's fine!" Maybe it wasn't a trap after all! Maybe she had actually believed me! For the first time I dared to hope that I could keep my secret. I was so astonished that I missed her next sentence. I only became aware that she was speaking again when I caught Miss Kellogg's name.

"She what?" I asked.

"She . . . listen, what are you doing this morning? Can I come over?"

"Sure. Come on."

"I'll be there in fifteen minutes," she said. "I'll tell you the whole story."

"Who was that?" Mom asked, as though she was grateful for the interruption.

"Lindy. She's coming over."

"Well, don't rush. Take your time and eat a decent breakfast."

Everything was settled about the Institute. There was nothing more for anyone to say. But when Sam passed my chair on his way into the den he whispered, "Cop-out!"

Lindy rang the doorbell just as I finished dressing. "It's freezing out!" she greeted me, offering her icy hands as proof. A little unsteadily, I took her coat and hung it in the hall closet. Perhaps she hadn't wanted to ask about last night over the phone. Perhaps she preferred to confront me in person.

I hustled her upstairs before she could ask Mom or Dad any polite questions about my grandmother's remarkable recovery. "You must have had a rough night last night," she said when we were settled in my room.

What did it matter, anyway? In a few more weeks I would be away at the Institute, and we wouldn't have to see each other anymore. Still, I asked carefully, "What makes you think so?"

"Well, you look like you didn't get much sleep, and you never even asked me about the opera."

"Oh no! I'm sorry—I meant to! How was it?"

She paused as though she weighed my reaction. "It was interesting. I can't say I was wild about it like Keith; it kind of dragged in places, but I wouldn't tell him that. The costumes were beautiful, and I liked some of the singing." She hesitated again. "But Miss Kellogg was—worse than usual."

"What do you mean, worse than usual?" I flared. "You're starting to sound like . . ."

"Listen, just let me tell you about it, and then you can tell me what you think." She sat down in the rocking chair by the window, and I dropped onto the bed. "First we went to this little fast-food place before we drove to New York. When we sat down she started whispering to us—we could hardly hear each other to begin with, there was such a racket in there —she started whispering something about the guy behind the counter looking at her funny. Finally she said that *they* were having her watched, and she was sure she'd seen him in front of her house a couple of times."

"But why would anyone . . ." I began.

"Wait. When we were on our way out we passed by that same guy, going out on his break or something. He was heading for the door the same time we were. All of a sudden Miss Kellogg turned around and yelled, 'Leave me alone! Stop following me or I'll call the police!' "

"Oh no!" I groaned. "She couldn't have said that! Maybe he said something to her that you didn't hear."

"It must have boggled his mind," Lindy went on relentlessly. "He kind of backed off, and we got her out of there quick. Not that I was all that eager to get back into the car with her, I can tell you. It was pretty spooky.

"Then all the way into the city she kept looking through the rearview mirror, thinking we were being followed. This green Plymouth was tailgating for a few miles. She got so nervous at the wheel I thought she was going to crack up the car!"

There was a diamond pattern in my quilt. My fingers traced and retraced the delicate threads that marked the boundary between two patches. "What did you say to her?"

"I kept trying to tell her not to worry, that it was nothing. Keith was great, he got her mind off it some, telling a bunch of funny stories. It got to where all we wanted was to get there in one piece."

I studied the pattern intently. The diamonds interlocked in so many ways, and no two pieces were alike. I hunted for my favorite patch, the satin.

"Are you listening?" Lindy demanded.

"Of course I'm listening!"

"Oh, I almost forgot. Somewhere along in there she told us about the paper."

"What paper?"

"The hundred reams for the *Messenger*. First the office said we had to get the cheapest grade, and only thirty reams, remember? That's when Miss Kellogg started saying how it wasn't fair, because the twirlers were getting new uniforms and all—well, she told us that one day she went into the office and the secretary in charge of supplies was absent, so she filled out a requisition sheet and gave it to the girl that was filling in, and told her Mr. Wallace said it was okay."

"You always said there was something strange about the way that paper turned up." I found the patch of satin. It was warm and smooth beneath my fingers.

"Now she thinks that's just one more reason for *them* to want to get rid of her. After listening to her talk about it long enough, I think I'm starting to believe her."

"On what grounds could they kick her out?"

"Take your pick. They're getting tons of complaints from kids and parents. Miss Kellogg doesn't follow the curriculum, she cheats on the order for paper— she doesn't obey the rules."

"Isn't there a teachers' union or something that could help her?"

"I guess so. But I don't know if she'll go to them. She said Mr. Wallace called her into his office last week and told her parents were complaining about some of the books she's been teaching— *Catcher in the Rye*'s supposed to be a dirty book or something— and some of the other teachers had complained that her classes are too noisy. He gave her a final warning."

"What does that mean?" I caught the edge of the quilt between my fingers and twisted it hard.

"I guess it means if anything else happens that he doesn't like, it'll be the last straw." The rhythmic creaking of the rocking chair filled the silence between us.

"She was nervous all through the show," Lindy went on finally. "I kept looking over at her and worrying—it gave me something to think about through the slow parts, anyway. I almost expected her to want to leave early, but I think she hung on for Keith. He was having the time of his life. He was so excited I don't think he registered half what Miss Kellogg said."

"How was the trip home?"

"A little better, I guess. At least she was quieter,

but that might've been because Keith was talking so much. Then when we were just coming into Ridge View and I was starting to think I'd misunderstood her after all, all of a sudden she said, 'If they check the records in Boston, they've got me for sure.' "

My scalp prickled. "What do you think she meant by that?"

"I don't know. What does it sound like to you?"

"She told me once she came from there. She left and came down here—she didn't really say why."

"It was the way she said they'd have her," Lindy reflected, "that makes me pretty sure she won't try to fight it through the union."

I opened my mouth to argue, but I had no words. I knew that Lindy was right. Miss Kellogg would not be at Ridge View High very much longer.

So I was right to leave school. Ridge View couldn't tolerate differences in people. They would drive us all out, me and Miss Kellogg and anyone else who didn't look or think like they did.

"Jeffrey Allen said last night his father's going to say something," I said, and then it was too late.

"Last night?" she asked into my confusion. "How come you saw Jeffrey last night?"

"I meant yesterday," I stumbled. But I was sure that she didn't believe me, even before she noticed my party dress, which still hung over my desk chair.

"This is beautiful." She rose and went to examine

it. Behind her the rocking chair bounced spasmod-
ically and was still. "You could have worn this to the
Met last night."

"I could have." She must know. But still I struggled to maintain the pretense. "I'm really sorry I had
to miss it."

"Me too." She edged toward the door. I felt her
pulling away from me, lied to, betrayed. "I promised
my mother I'd come straight home," she was saying.
"She wants me to watch my little sister." And she
was going, expecting me to see her to the door, to exchange polite good-byes. . . .

"Lindy . . ."

"What?" She turned back.

I couldn't hope that she might still want me for a
friend, but if I made a full confession maybe I could
rid myself of this awful heavy feeling in my chest.

"Lindy," I tried again, with her full attention now.
But the words knotted together, they formed a solid,
unyielding lump in my throat. "I hope everything'll
work out for the best," I choked.

"I sure do too!"

Downstairs I got her coat from the closet, and we
said good-bye at the front door. When she had gone,
I still had that feeling in my chest.

12

On Monday, the Christmas spirit had infected Ridge View High. Mr. Wallace opened the morning announcements with a jolly "Merry Christmas!" to teachers and students. The public-address system poured carols into the halls between classes. In the cafeteria Lindy and I sampled a sweet, chewy substance that was billed as plum pudding.

Someday soon I would walk through the cafeteria line for the last time. Soon I would have to tell Lindy that I was leaving. At any moment she would demand to know what I had really done on Friday night. Oppressed by my unspoken thoughts, I had nothing to say to her when we sat at our accustomed table in the corner. Lindy, too, seemed abstracted, and we limped into a forlorn discussion about what I should buy Dad for Christmas.

So when Keith rushed up to us, I was so grateful for the interruption that in the first instant I didn't hear what he was saying. Then his words crashed in around me.

"They're going to fire Miss Kellogg!"

Then Lindy and I were talking at once. Who said so? It couldn't be true! We were afraid something like this would happen, but why? Over our racket Keith kept pleading, "Listen, will you? Let me tell you!" until at last we grew quiet and gave him our complete attention.

"You know that wise guy Jeffrey Allen that all the girls think is so cool?"

Lindy and I murmured our assent. Yes, we knew Jeffrey Allen. I dropped my hands to my lap where no one could see how tightly they clenched.

"Well, in gym fourth period he was walking around the locker room bragging how he and his father went in this morning and told some story to Wallace, how Miss Kellogg insulted Jeffrey in front of the class, called him a—a philistine, I think it was. And Wallace got real ticked off and dragged her in there and . . ."

"They can't fire her just for that!" I said. "Anyway, Jeffrey really is . . ."

"Will you just let me finish? They got her back there into Wallace's inner sanctum, and when Wallace asked her about this thing with Jeffrey I guess she kind of freaked out. I mean, the way Jeffrey was talking, it sounds like she got hysterical. She said they were all against her and she didn't have a chance, said Wallace had no right to go through her drawers and tap her phone and have her house watched . . ."

"Oh no!" Lindy groaned. "She really blew it!"

"It must have been a terrible scene. Jeffrey said she was so upset Wallace had him and his father wait outside. Then after he talked to her alone a while Wallace called Jeffery's father back in and said they'd known Miss Kellogg had had a breakdown in Boston on some other teaching job, and they had been watching her for problems—and they were asking her to resign."

"They can't do that!" I cried, knowing that they could, and that they would.

"That's only what Jeffrey was saying fourth period," Keith tried to reassure me. "He might've made the whole thing up, knowing him."

"Come on," Lindy broke in. "You saw her Friday night. If she acted like that in Wallace's office, in front of some kid's father, he'd have to fire her."

"And Jeffrey's father's on the Town Council," I said.

"I wonder if she'll be in class this afternoon," Lindy said. The bell rang. We stacked our trays and joined the throng in the halls. From the speakers above our heads poured a lively rendition of "Deck the Halls With Boughs of Holly."

"She's still here." We took our seats and Lindy leaned toward me across the aisle. "She looks nervous, though."

The bell rang again, and "Deck the Halls" broke off in the middle of a fa-la-la. The murmur of talk ebbed slowly. Chalk scratched on the front blackboard.

Footsteps hurried down the aisle toward me. "Hi, Meg!" Karen said, her giggle sparkling through her lowered voice. "You recovered yet from the other night?"

She spoke softly, but I knew that Lindy had heard her. I didn't answer. As though nothing had happened, Karen breezed back to her seat.

Miss Kellogg shut the door and turned to the class. "all in green went my love riding on a great horse of gold into the silver dawn. . . ."

For the past two weeks, she had devoted every class period to sentence structure and the parts of speech. Now a lump grew in my throat as she read the lines she had copied onto the blackboard. "four lean hounds crouched low and smiling the silver deer fled before . . ." The haunting words filled me with the horror of the chase—the anguish of the deer, the relentless cruelty of the hunter and the hounds.

". . . four lean hounds crouched low and smiling my heart fell dead before."

A long silence shimmered behind the final lines, two seconds, three seconds. Then, with slow, deliberate strokes, Miss Kellogg's eraser swept the blackboard clean. "Now," she said, "who can tell me what an infinitive phrase is?"

The rules of usage clattered around me, shaking me loose from the sadness the poem had awakened. With half of my attention on gerunds and infinitives, I thought about Lindy and what I would have to tell her when the bell rang. I should have told her the truth in my room on Saturday. Now I had compounded my lie by vainly trying to keep my secret. Anyway, I reminded myself, I was going to leave Ridge View High. Miss Kellogg and I would be driven away like the deer by the lean smiling hounds. No one understood us. No one wanted to understand.

The class dragged, as slow and dull as Mrs. Keene's history class. Karen couldn't think of a sentence containing a gerund. Like any ordinary teacher, Miss Kellogg left her searching and stammering, and selected another victim. Harry Wilson mumbled that he didn't know either. I could guess what Miss Kellogg was thinking. This is how you want me to teach; I'll give you what you deserve. But I wished that the class would never end. As soon as the bell rang, I would have to tell Lindy why Karen had asked me if I had recovered from the other night.

"I have an announcement to make." Miss Kellogg's words shattered my reverie. "This is the last class I will teach you. This morning I turned in my resignation."

I had thought that I was prepared. Since Saturday I had been telling myself that Miss Kellogg and I were destined to leave Ridge View High together as fellow outcasts. But now her words stunned me. Amazed and outraged, I heard the excited whispers spring up through the room, and Miss Kellogg's voice above them, stony, matter-of-fact. "I'm resigning because I can't teach here. You've all seen to that. You were afraid of the things I offered you. You don't want anyone to make you think." Her voice rose, and the stoniness melted into passion. "I'm going of my own free will, do you understand? I'm going by choice, before you drive me out. I won't stay in a place like this, where they plot to get rid of me. I've given what I can." Her voice dropped, nearly broke. "It's time for me to be going."

The bell rang. Shakily I rose and went through the motions of gathering my books. Beside me Lindy murmured, "She looked like she was going to cry."

"Wait," I said, before we reached the door. "I want to talk to her a minute."

"She's already gone," Lindy said. I took her arm and we stepped into the corridor. "Deck the Halls" had resumed where it had been cut off. "Maybe we can catch up with her."

But Lindy couldn't see her anywhere. Miss Kellogg had escaped into the crowd. "Listen," Lindy said, "there isn't time to talk here. Meet me at three o'clock, okay?"

We had reached the branch in the hall where our paths divided. "Okay," I said. "By my locker. Three o'clock."

My Spanish class had practiced for two weeks, and that afternoon we went caroling through the halls. I tried to sing at first, but I felt so overcome with sadness when I heard the clear, gentle Spanish words that I fell silent. I walked along with the procession, outside it, not even listening. It was true. Miss Kellogg was really leaving, and Jeffrey Allen had provided the last straw that Mr. Wallace had needed. I marveled that the thought of Jeffrey had ever set my heart pounding. I didn't feel anything for him now. I could hardly remember how I had ever cared about him so much.

Miss Kellogg had resigned. The thought revolved back into focus. Tomorrow there would be a substitute teacher in front of the room, some inept stranger pretending to take her place. The students, the other teachers, Mr. Wallace—none of them had ever really appreciated Miss Kellogg. She had always said it— they didn't want to think, and she frightened them. But she hadn't been content to let them rest in their conformity. She had tried to jar them into some kind of realization, and they had fought back.

It wasn't fair. She was the best teacher any of us had ever had, and she had been hurt so often that by now she distrusted practically everyone. People thought that she was crazy, and maybe she was, but she had been pushed into that world of fears and suspicions.

Anger was thrusting my sadness aside. I couldn't sit by passively and let this happen. I would do something. I would make all of Ridge View High recognize this injustice.

As we passed the study hall, alive with the rustle of pages, I joined the singing again. *"Noche de paz, noche de amor . . ."* I felt a little taller, lifting my voice with the others. I would do something for Miss Kellogg, no matter what anyone thought of me for it.

The three-o'clock bell rang. Calling *adios* behind me, I rushed to my locker to meet Lindy.

"Listen," I greeted her, a little breathless from the running and from the tumult in my head, "we've got to do something for Miss Kellogg!"

"How do you mean?" she asked.

"We can't let them force her out. We need her here."

I found my key and twisted open the padlock while Lindy reflected. "I think it's too late for that," she said. "She has to go now, after all the stuff that's happened."

"We'll organize a protest, a student strike . . ."

"With who?" She laughed bitterly. "With all the kids who wanted her out in the first place?"

Deflated, I sorted out my books. I pulled on my coat and banged the metal door shut. "Let's go see her, anyway. At least we can go and . . ." I couldn't bring myself to think of saying good-bye. "At least we can talk to her and figure out what to do."

But Room Two Thirty-four was closed and locked. "The lights are out, too," Lindy said. "She must have gone home already."

I stood with my hand on the doorknob. I couldn't think what to do next.

"I wonder what we'll do about the *Messenger*," Lindy said.

"We can go ahead, can't we? We've got the paper and the layout, and Mr. Baranowski promised to print it the week we get back from vacation."

"All we need now is the editorial," Lindy said.

"That's it!" I cried. "Why didn't I think of it? Let's write an editorial, in protest!"

"We'd get expelled," Lindy argued.

"Just for expressing our opinion? There's freedom of the press."

"Not in this school," Lindy stated. "I'm thirsty."

Still talking, I followed her to the fountain at the end of the hall. "We could really shame all those people who made her resign. They can't just get away with it."

Lindy didn't answer. Water splashed in the basin.

"I'm already coming up with ideas for it," I went on. "We should write it together, though, and let's get Keith in on it too."

"You want some water?" Lindy asked, straightening.

"What's the matter? You're not even listening."

"I am too. I don't know—maybe Wallace *had* to do it. She was getting so—you know, I told you about the opera."

"Yes, but would she have gotten like that in the first place if people hadn't rejected her in the beginning just for being different?"

"Maybe not. But anyway, we'd really catch it."

"You're not scared, are you?" I was astounded. "You never worried about rules before. They probably never even wrote one about anything like this."

"It's easy for you not to worry," she said. "They wouldn't do anything to you anyway."

"Come on, they won't do anything to any of us." But they couldn't do anything to punish me. I would be leaving soon, going to the Institute.

"Well, I can see your point. Miss Kellogg would approve, I know that much."

"I feel like we owe it to her," I said.

"Oh, I suppose you're right."

"You mean you'll do it?" I cried.

"You knew you could talk me into it."

Lindy paused. In my excitement over the plan, I was completely unprepared when she asked, "By the way, what was Karen talking about this afternoon, something about had you recovered from the other night?"

I gripped the cold porcelain rim of the drinking fountain. Of course she hadn't forgotten. Of course I would have to tell her now, just when we had become fellow conspirators, and now she would want nothing more to do with my editorial—or my friendship.

"I didn't want to tell you this," I began. "I was kind of afraid you'd—Well—my grandmother wasn't really sick the other night. I didn't go to the Met with you guys because I went to a party at Karen's instead."

I stopped, waiting for the explosion of anger and condemnation I deserved.

"You went to a party at Karen's!" Lindy repeated. "Why the heck did you do a dumb thing like that?"

I had no answer. I still gripped the fountain, waiting for the tirade. I was ready to beg for forgiveness, to plead that I had learned my lesson.

"I bet you had a lousy time," Lindy went on. "The

opera got pretty boring, but it couldn't be as bad as a whole night with all those snotty kids!"

"It was bad, all right." I managed a nervous laugh.

"But why did you do it?" she repeated. She didn't sound angry, just puzzled.

"When she invited me," I began haltingly, "I thought how that's the kind of party everybody goes to, everybody but me, it seemed like. I had to find out what it would be like. It felt real important at the time. I hated to miss the opera after we'd been planning it for so long, but I couldn't turn down that chance."

"I guess everybody goes through that sooner or later." Lindy hesitated. "Last year I went to one of their parties the night my dog Tippy was dying. I still can't believe I was so stupid."

"You did?" I could hardly believe it. "I thought you always went your own way and never cared what people thought."

"I wouldn't want to go to one of their parties now," she said. "Anyway, they never invite me anymore. All they do is sit around and gossip about everybody that's not there, and drink beer . . ."

"And think they're adults just because they're playing kissing games!"

"Didn't you hate it? I felt so silly being there, after about an hour I decided not to talk to anybody. So the whole rest of the time I didn't say a word, just sat and watched them. Why didn't you tell me?"

"I was afraid you'd think I was one of *them*," I confessed.

We both giggled. I gave her a quick hug and stepped back, laughing with relief. "We better not tell Keith," she said. "He wouldn't understand even wanting to try a party like that, especially if it meant missing Beverly Sills."

"Promise you won't tell him!" I begged.

"Promised," she said. "But let's get him to help with the editorial."

"You really want to do it?"

"I told you you talked me into it."

"Oh no!" I cried suddenly. "Today's Monday! I'm supposed to be seeing Mrs. Gomez!"

"Well, I'd about given up on you." Mrs. Gomez met me in the doorway. "I was getting ready to leave."

"I'm sorry," I gasped. "I was doing a bunch of different things—I guess I forgot."

Mrs. Gomez hesitated. "It's already three-thirty. We only have half an hour left to work."

I braced myself for the scolding that was coming—how did I expect to pass algebra if I didn't even make use of the tutoring she offered? It was my responsibility, after all. . . .

"Would you mind if we skip this afternoon?" she asked. "You're doing very well. I'm sure it won't hurt—

and I have to pick up my daughter at the airport. I could get a slightly earlier start."

"You have a daughter?" It had never occurred to me that Mrs. Gomez had a family, a home, a life that had nothing to do with sets and formulas.

"I have two daughters," she told me. "Cynthia's the oldest. She hasn't been feeling well lately and now they think she's got mononucleosis, so she's coming home from college, taking incompletes in all her subjects. We'll see—I don't think those doctors at the college clinic know anything."

I tried to imagine Cynthia, a girl who, since her infancy, had called Mrs. Gomez *Mom*. It was almost inconceivable. But Mrs. Gomez sounded exactly like someone's mother, worrying about whether the doctor really knew the right things to do for her poor daughter. "It's okay with me if we don't work today," I said. "It was my fault for being late anyway."

"We'll still have a few more sessions to review before your midyear exam," she said. We stepped into the hall and she locked the door behind us. "If you really work, I'll be surprised if you get anything lower than a B."

"A B!" I exclaimed. "I just keep hoping I'll pass."

"You could be a B student if you put your mind to it," she promised.

Wouldn't Mom and Dad be pleased if I actually got a B in algebra, if I could show them so unques-

tionably that things were really working out? But I
had decided to go to the Institute. After this midyear
exam, I wouldn't have to worry about things working
out any longer.

I clattered down Stairway C and past the girls' gym.
Even through the closed door I could hear a vigorous
cheering practice in session, and for a moment I
paused to listen. "Get that ball and *go*, team! Get that
ball and *go*, team!" The strident voices rang with enthusiasm for a common cause. I could tell they were
having fun.

But Lindy and Keith and I and the others who had
worked on the *Messenger* had a common cause, too.
It was a less popular cause than the winning of basket-
ball games, but it had its own elements of fun and
challenge. They were chanting "*De*-fense! *De*-fense!"
as I continued down the hall, but for the first time I
didn't feel even a pang of envy.

As I rounded a corner, I heard one of the janitors
mopping the floor ahead. I slowed my steps, extending
my cane to search for the inevitable bucket. "Careful,
Miss!" he exclaimed. "Easy does it!" His voice was
shaky with age.

The mop handle tapped the floor as he took my arm
and led me on a wide detour. "They say we're in for a
blizzard," he said, releasing my arm when we were
past the danger.

"You think we'll get it?"

"We don't get snow like we used to," he said. "I remember when you'd wake up and you couldn't see the tops of the fences. Seems to me like all these rockets they keep shooting up there must affect the weather somehow or other." He retrieved the mop and sloshed it in the pail.

"I never thought of that," I said. It sounded far-fetched, but he might be right after all.

"Ask your science teacher," he urged, pushing the mop across the floor in a wet swath. "You might get him working on it."

"Somebody ought to look into it," I told him.

"You know, most of the kids just think I'm a nut," he said in parting. "I talk to them and they walk the other way. So long, Miss."

The swish of the mop faded behind me. I imagined what would have happened if I had refused his help and struggled past him alone. He would have watched me tensely, afraid to give me directions, certainly unwilling to open a conversation. I would never have found out what he thought about the space program's effects on the climate.

It was hard to remember that in February I would leave all of this and enter the Institute. I had learned a lot at Ridge View High.

valuable teacher. The students have lost a rare opportunity for learning.

"But even worse, we fear that a dangerous precedent
has been established, an intolerance for dissent. It is
the school's responsibility to encourage open-minded-
ness in its students, to help them develop the capacity
for clear thinking. If the school teaches that those
who are different, who will not or cannot conform,
must be rejected, what kind of society does it seek to
create?"

"Wow!" Lindy sighed. "It sure does tell it like it
is!"

"I think that's what I've been wanting to say for a
while now." I wondered if Keith and Lindy guessed
that I had not only written my section in defense of
Miss Kellogg; somehow I had been trying to claim my
own right to be different too. "I wish we could read
it to Miss Kellogg," I said, biting into the gingerbread
man at last.

"Maybe she's in the phone book," Keith said. "Let's
call her up."

The droning roar of Mom's vacuum cleaner grew
louder as she started on the living room. I lifted the
fat directory down from the pantry shelf, and Keith
and Lindy pored over the K's. There were fifteen Kel-
loggs in Ridge View, but no listing of a Frances. There
was an F. L., but an old man answered and said he'd
lived alone since his wife passed on.

"She probably has an unlisted number," Lindy said. "She wouldn't want *them* to track her down."

"No, she wouldn't," I agreed. For the first time I realized that I might never see Miss Kellogg again.

The day we returned from Christmas vacation, Mr. Sirovich announced that he was Miss Kellogg's permanent replacement. "That's S-I-R-O-V-I-C-H," he declared. "So if you're moved to commemorate me in graffiti, please spell it right." He referred to Homer's epics as "the Idiot and the Oddity," and said that a composition should be like a woman's skirt, "long enough to cover the subject, but short enough to be interesting." Everyone laughed. I could tell that he was destined to become one of the popular teachers at Ridge View High.

When the period was nearly over, he reached into a desk drawer and held something up for the class's inspection. "Does anyone have an idea what this is?" he asked. "It looks like hieroglyphics."

I could have told him what it was, but I guarded Miss Kellogg's secret. Just as she had foreseen, her drawers were being searched, and just as she had intended, no one could decipher her messages.

Mr. Sirovich insisted that we proceed with our original plans for the *Messenger*. He unlocked the supply closet for us, and even helped us carry the paper down to the printing department in the basement. We delivered ninety-eight reams to Mr. Baranowski, and he began work on the magazine that same afternoon.

Lindy's older brother had a small printing press in his garage, and we only wasted a few sheets from the two reams we had held aside before it started turning out good clear copies of the editorial. On Friday Mr. Baranowski finished the printing, and we carried the boxes of loose pages up to Room Two Thirty-four for the final sorting and stapling and for the insertion of the editorial between the Table of Contents and Page 1. Mr. Sirovich wandered in and out, eager for us to finish so he could begin his weekend. He did leaf through one of the finished copies, but if he noticed anything unusual about it, he didn't say so to us.

On Monday morning we left a neat stack of *Messengers* in the school bookstore and distributed the rest among the various homerooms, where they were available to anyone who wished to look at them.

All morning I waited for something to happen, though I hardly knew what I expected. I felt strangely alert and capable, prepared for anything.

But the announcement didn't come until sixth period was almost over. Mr. Wallace had abandoned his usual joviality. The voice over the public-address system crackled with authority. "This is an important announcement to all teachers. Any copies of the school magazine, the *Messenger*, which have not as yet been distributed should be held until three o'clock and turned in at the main office. I repeat, this is an important announcement. . . ."

"The *Messenger*, eh?" Mr. Sirovich sounded bemused. "Has anybody seen it? What is it, porno?"

"It's the editorial," Warren explained. "It's about Miss Kellogg, that they shouldn't have kicked her out."

The clamor that arose rivaled the noisiest moments of Miss Kellogg's class. Those who had read the editorial shouted out their impressions, and those who had not read it demanded to see it at once. "Hey, you two work on the *Messenger*," Mr. Sirovich called to us over the din. "What do you know about all this?"

There was no time for us to compose an answer. The telephone buzzed, and Mr. Sirovich reported, "Meg Hollis, Lindy Blake, you're wanted at headquarters."

We were celebrities as we rose and walked to the door, pursued by eager questions and bits of advice. "Just remember you've got the First Amendment on your side," Mr. Sirovich said before he shut the door behind us.

"I don't know if anybody gets our message," I said, "but at least we're creating a stir."

"We better get our act down," Lindy cautioned. "What'll we say?"

"What can we tell him but the truth? We signed our names to it."

"That part wasn't my idea," Lindy said. "Well, now we're all in it together."

Keith was there ahead of us. We could hear Mr. Wallace questioning him as we passed the clattering typewriters. "Yes," Keith was saying as we stepped into the carpeted inner office, "I was aware what I was doing." His voice was steady.

"Sit down, girls," Mr. Wallace greeted us. "We have to discuss a matter of some importance." He paused for impact, tapping the glass desk top with what sounded like a sheaf of papers. "Are you responsible for this editorial that appeared in the *Messenger*?"

"Yes," I said, and Lindy echoed, "Yes, we wrote it."

The boldness of our admission surprised and angered him. He tried again to frighten us. "Do you realize that you're meddling in affairs that don't concern you? You're making statements in this editorial of yours that are just plain untrue." He flipped over a few pages and read indignantly, " 'Students, teachers, parents, and school administrators were dismayed by some of Miss Kellogg's views. As a direct result, she has been forced to resign.' What have you got to say for yourselves?"

"Sir," Keith began, polite but firm, "everything we said there seems to us to be true."

"You can't make a public statement like that without knowing the facts." Mr. Wallace got up and paced the room. He rolled up the *Messenger* and tapped it against his hand. "I've had two teachers come in to me already today demanding to know just why Miss Kellogg resigned. You've got people thinking that I asked her to leave because I disagreed with her! You've spread this rumor through the whole school that I've committed some gross injustice. Doesn't that mean anything to you?"

"We didn't mean to mislead anybody," I said. "We just wanted people to think about what had happened."

"What happened, if you must involve yourselves in administrative decisions, was that Miss Kellogg had some very serious emotional problems that made her unfit for her teaching duties." He stopped beside my chair, looming over me. "Her resignation was in her own best interest, and in the best interests of her students. In fact, I assured her that we would welcome her back if she receives—the medical attention she needs."

He ignored the bell and went on, "Now do you understand why I'm disturbed by what you've done? You've created a very bad atmosphere here, a lot of mistrust."

None of us said anything. Of course he would never admit that her views had anything to do with Miss Kellogg's resignation. Of course he could fall back on the excuse that she was too sick to teach. But students and parents had begun to complain to him back in September, before anyone had thought of her as mentally unbalanced, simply because she didn't follow the curriculum and seemed to demand too much from her classes. I couldn't separate the two elements.

"What you three have done requires disciplinary measures." Mr. Wallace paced back to his desk and sat down. "I'll have to notify your parents. Will you give me your telephone number, Mr. Howard?"

"Five five five, eight nine eight four, but nobody's home right now. . . ."

"Miss Blake?"

A little shakily, Lindy gave him the number. I wished I could reassure her somehow, but with Mr. Wallace looking on there was no way for us to communicate.

"Meg?" For the first time, Mr. Wallace seemed to remember who I was. "I'm sorry to see you involved in all this. I hate to have to worry your folks. . . ."

"Five five five, one four one six," I interrupted.

"That's all for right now." He stood up and opened the door. The rattle of the typewriters and the ringing of a telephone poured into the room. "The secretary will write late passes for you."

Eager to escape from the office, I rose with the others. I couldn't wait to exchange thoughts and impressions with them. But Mr. Wallace laid a restraining hand on my shoulder. "Stay a minute, Meg. I want to speak to you."

I sat down again, my hands clenched. I knew what was coming, and I detested it. Lindy and Keith and I were in this together, but I was being separated from them, to be given some special consideration. "Talk to you after school," I called to their retreating footsteps, but Mr. Wallace closed the door again before they could answer.

"Listen, Meg." His voice was no longer stern. "I hate to see you dragged into this. Did those kids read you that editorial before they put your name on it?"

"I helped write it." My right hand closed around the cold metal of the chair arm. "It was my idea to begin with."

"But they influenced you, didn't they? You wouldn't have done a thing like that on your own."

"You don't understand. I talked them into it. It was my idea."

He stopped, taken aback. "But you're not like some of these kids we get, the real rabble-rousers. I know you must have liked Miss Kellogg—don't misunderstand me, we all liked her. If she gets the help she needs, she could be a fine teacher. But some of what you call her unconventional ideas were really just the result of her sickness. That's hard for a person your age to grasp, I know. You were doing what you thought was right, weren't you?"

"We were expressing our opinion," I said. "It was freedom of the press, like in the First Amendment. If we're wrong, then you can tell your side of it some-how. . . ."

"That would be very—inconvenient. I can't exactly get on the P.A. and announce to the whole school that I asked Miss Kellogg to resign because she was having a nervous breakdown. The decisions that are made in this office aren't open for review by the public." He struck a match, and for a moment I caught its acrid smell. "If we keep things quiet, this will all blow over by the end of the week. . . . Let me tell you some-thing. Frankly, I think I ought to be lenient with you. After all, you haven't been in trouble before. I know your folks have been concerned about your adjust-ment here. If they felt you were getting swept along by the wrong crowd, getting crazy ideas in your head, it might upset them. We're all inspired by how well you've been doing here. I'd hate to see your family decide to pull you out."

Just last week we had filled out my application to the Institute for the Blind. I had already decided to leave Ridge View High, to give up the struggle. But Mr. Wallace's words touched some vulnerable spot within me. He was right. I didn't want him to upset

Mom and Dad with this story. I wanted to tell them I had changed my mind, that I would stay here after all. Maybe I had known all along that I didn't ever really want to leave.

"You see, you may have a lot at stake." Mr. Wallace seemed to sense his advantage. "As I say, I don't have to call your parents. This little talk today should be enough to set you straight on this kind of thing in the future. Now, you're missing your seventh-period class."

We both stood up. In a daze I followed him through the door. "You think about it," he said. "You seem to understand the issues involved."

I thought about it through the rest of the afternoon.

Mrs. Gomez must have known all along what was on my mind, but she waited until I had hopelessly tangled three equations before she commented, "I read your editorial this morning."

"You did?" I rested my hands on the meaningless page in front of me. "What did you think?"

"I thought it was about time somebody spoke out about some of the things that go on around here. Not that anybody'll listen to you, any more than they listened to Frances Kellogg."

Through my amazement I found myself answering, "I wish we could get in touch with Miss Kellogg somehow. I didn't even have a chance to say good-bye when she left. I could at least write to her."

"I'll look up her address for you in the office," Mrs. Gomez said. "That's easy enough. Has Mr. Wallace talked to you yet?"

"He's real mad," I told her. "He says Miss Kellogg didn't have to leave because of her ideas, that she had to leave because she had emotional problems."

"I've seen some pretty crazy teachers kept on here for years and years," Mrs. Gomez said. "As long as they didn't step on any toes. I take it you're in hot water right now."

"I don't know what to do," I blurted. "Mr. Wallace says he won't call my parents if I don't want him to, and I don't want to get suspended or anything because they might get worried and want me to leave this school. But Lindy and Keith and I, we were all in this together, and they're getting into all kinds of trouble."

"Are you asking for my opinion?" I had the feeling she would give it to me whether I asked for it or not. "You better take the same punishment those other kids get, or you'll never forgive yourself."

I had known that, even during the roughest moments in Mr. Wallace's office. But hearing Mrs. Gomez put it into words made everything suddenly clear and simple. "What about my parents?" I asked.

"Well, you know them better than I do," she said. "But they seemed like reasonable people when I met them. You'll just have to tell them the story, that's all."

"Is it okay if we stop for this afternoon?" I asked. "I can't think about math right now. If I hurry, maybe I can catch Mr. Wallace before he leaves."

"You better run." She walked with me to the door. "He leaves pretty early sometimes."

"I will. Thanks." I couldn't wait another moment. I had to find him, had to set things right with Lindy and Keith. I ran.

"Is Mr. Wallace here?" I leaned against the glass-topped counter, breathless and urgent.

"Meg." He stood only a few feet away. "You want to speak to me about something?"

"I think you better call my parents." I tried to steady my voice, but the words sounded jagged. "I think I better get whatever punishment you decide on for Keith and Lindy."

"Are you sure that's what you want?" He sounded nonplussed. "I've got my coat on, I was just leaving. We can talk about this some more tomorrow if you want to . . ."

"There isn't anything to talk about. If you're calling their parents, you have to call mine."

Behind the counter the typewriters fell silent. "There may be an alternative," he said. "You know how I feel about . . ."

"There's only one alternative I can think of," I said. "You could treat them like you want to treat me —I mean, you could be lenient with them, too. It's *their* first time in trouble, it's going to upset *their* parents . . ."

"No, I'm sorry, that really isn't possible." He turned away. "You don't give me any choice then, Meg. I hope you won't regret this decision."

The air outside was very cold but still, the unnatural calm before a storm. As I walked home through the familiar streets I pictured the telephone ringing in the kitchen, and Mom's growing anxiety as Mr. Wallace gave her his version of what had happened. If she was worried enough, she might call Dad at the office. I tried to plan what I would say. I would have to be pretty eloquent this time to convince them that I should stay at Ridge View High after all. There were so many things they might not understand.

But I couldn't concentrate on my speech. The air seemed to freeze my thoughts, and it required all my energy just to climb the hill. I would have to rely on my intuition when the time came.

But not for one minute did I regret my decision.

I turned right at the corner of Prospect Street, and in two minutes more I was on the front porch fitting my key to the lock.

14

I found Mom in the kitchen, unpacking a load of groceries. "How's your day been?" she asked.

"Fine." Could she already have talked to Mr. Wallace? "How was yours?"

"Well, I drove out to the Mall to pick up some fabric on sale this afternoon, and wound up stuck in a traffic jam for forty-five minutes. I just got home."

"Any phone calls?" I asked, just to be sure.

"Oh, right. Lindy called. You're supposed to call her back as soon as you get in."

I helped her put the groceries away, waiting until

she was out of the kitchen before I picked up the phone. I was certain that Mr. Wallace would try to call this afternoon or tonight, but now at least I could prepare Mom for the shock. Still, I could call Lindy first. It wouldn't hurt to tie up the phone for a little while.

Mrs. Blake answered with a brusque hello, and cupped her hand over the mouthpiece when she recognized my voice. Through a distorted jumble of talk I thought I caught my own name, and something that sounded like "three days." Then Lindy said, "Meg, listen, I'm in the middle of a pretty tense scene over here, I can't talk long."

"Wallace called?"

"He burned my mother's ear off! Said I was sticking my nose into things that were none of my business, trying to break down student-teacher relations —my folks are quite upset. Oh yeah, I'm suspended for three days, and so is Keith."

"I am too," I told her.

"That's why he had that little talk with you after we left?" I had never heard that note of sarcasm in her voice before. "My father just got home, and Mom's in the other room filling him in . . ."

"I *am* suspended!" I insisted. "I told him he'd have to either let us all off or punish me too. I'm not copping out."

"You're really suspended too?"

"Well, Mom was out, so he hasn't called yet, but he will. I'll get suspended too, you'll see."

"That shouldn't make me feel better," she said, "but it does. I was pretty mad at you, you know, that it was your idea but you wouldn't get into trouble for it. Do you think we got our point across to anybody with the editorial, though?"

"Lots of people had a chance to read it. Hey, you won't believe it, but even Mrs. Gomez saw it, and she was actually human about it all. . . ."

"Rosalind!" Even over the wires, her father's voice was jarring.

"I've got to hang up," she whispered. "I'll call you later. 'Bye."

I still felt a little uneasy about calling a boy, even Keith, but I decided to keep the line busy a little longer, and dialed his number. "How are things going at your house?" I demanded when he answered. "Did Wallace talk to your parents yet?"

"Oh, that," he said. "My father's been reminiscing for the past half hour about all the trouble he got into when he was a kid. He thought the editorial was tremendous, but I told him you wrote most of it. Hey, guess what! I'm suspended for the next three days!"

"Me too!"

"Great! Hey, let's do something. We can go into the city for a Wednesday matinee if your folks'll let you."

"Oh let's—if I can. I don't know. They haven't heard yet." Mom's steps approached across the dining room. "I'll try. Think I better go now though. 'Bye."

The phone rang seconds after I set down the receiver, one loud ring that tightened my stomach and set my heart racing. "Hello," Mr. Wallace said. "Meg, may I speak with your father or mother?"

I thought of telling him that he had the wrong number, or saying that I was home alone. But he had recognized my voice, and Mom stood listening beside me. "Just a minute," I said. I whispered, "Mom, I'll explain everything. It's Mr. Wallace."

"Hello, Mr. Wallace." Mom's voice was casual, revealing nothing. "No, no she hasn't. . . . Oh, really?" Her tone rose. "Well, I'm sure they didn't mean to— I understand that, but— Yes. Yes, of course I will. . . . I suppose so, if the others are too. All right. Good-bye."

"Meg," she said, stepping toward me, "what's this all about? Mr. Wallace is very upset. He says you signed your name to some kind of incriminating editorial in the school magazine."

"I was going to tell you about it, honest. It's not like he says. I can show you the editorial; I've got a copy of the *Messenger*."

"Mr. Wallace says you're suspended. You're not to go to school for three days."

"Thank goodness!" I exclaimed, and added hastily,

"I mean, that he's suspending me too, along with Keith and Lindy. I decided . . ."

A key turned in the front door, and Dad whistled his customary greeting, the opening bars to "Oklahoma." His briefcase thumped down in the vestibule. "Anybody home?"

"Don't mention this to your father till he's had a chance to relax," Mom warned. "He went to court on the Ellison case this morning."

Mom hurried to take Dad's coat, to offer him a cocktail with some cheese and crackers, to inquire about the Ellison case. So it wasn't until we were all assembled around the dinner table that I could tell my story.

Dad asked me to say the Grace. I folded my hands on the edge of the table and recited, "Lord we come to Thee at this time to thank Thee for our blessings. We thank Thee for our health and strength and happiness amen." Before anyone had a chance to break in with talk about passing the salt, I rushed on, "I want to tell you why Mr. Wallace called before. It has to do with Miss Kellogg having to resign. . . ."

They were a good audience, interrupting now and then with questions and exclamations, but staying with me until I arrived at the end of the story, in Mr. Wallace's office. "So that's why we all got suspended," I concluded. "And I'm glad he suspended me too."

"You never told us about any of this." I thought Mom sounded a little wistful.

"I guess maybe I should have." There was a short, awkward pause. "Well, do you want to see what we wrote?"

Reading during meals was generally forbidden at our house, but tonight was an exception. I brought out the *Messenger*, and from the head of the table Dad read the editorial aloud. I gnawed on a chicken drumstick, trying to be calm, but I had no appetite. I heard every word from their point of view, and suddenly what we had written seemed overstated and irrelevant. We should have presented more facts, we should have prepared stronger arguments.

At last Dad put the magazine down. "They don't go in much for freedom of expression at that school, do they?" Dad asked. "Judging by the way Mr. Wallace reacted to your editorial, I wouldn't be surprised if he did get rid of Miss Kellogg because she disagreed with him."

"It sounds like she has got some problems, though," Mom said. "Maybe for her own sake it's just as well she's away from that situation and can get some help now. Still, you're going to miss her a lot, I bet."

"She was—special." I couldn't find a better word to describe her.

"I bet I wouldn't have had the guts to write something like that and put my name on it," Sam said.

Then, on second thought, he amended, "But you didn't have to worry about getting into trouble. You're leaving that school anyway."

I took a deep breath. "I'm not leaving," I said. "I changed my mind. I decided to stay at Ridge View."

"Are you sure this is what you really want?" Dad broke the stunned silence. "You really haven't been happy there, have you?"

"No, not always." I thought hard. "I guess nobody's happy all the time anywhere. I've made friends here, I'm learning a lot—I really do want to stay."

"It's so hard for us to know," Mom said. "We don't want to see you hurt."

"I can't go through life without getting hurt once in a while," I said.

"You still have time to think this over," Dad reminded me. "Your application is in. You can go to the Institute if you decide . . ."

"That's what I'm telling you!" I exclaimed. "I *have* decided. When I said I wanted to leave, I was just upset about something. Deep down, I guess I always wanted to stay. Everything's just beginning."

"Maybe in another year or two," Dad went on, as though he hadn't heard me, "maybe by then you'll feel more ready . . ."

"This is getting boring," Sam announced. "She said she made up her mind. So, she's not a cop-out. How come nobody's listening?"

"Well," Mom said. "Nobody knows how you feel but you, Meg. You're old enough to know what you want."

"I know what I want," I repeated. Everyone was becoming too serious. "Hey, you never said what you thought of the editorial?"

"I can see why the principal is so mad," Dad said. "You probably should have made sure you had all the facts . . ."

"Well, I'm proud of you," Mom interrupted. "You did the right thing."

"I was getting to that," Dad protested. "I was going to say I didn't think any of you kids deserved to be suspended, but you knew that was a possibility when you started out. Mr. Wallace makes the rules."

"I think you better eat your dinner," Mom said finally. "It's getting cold, and you haven't taken three bites."

Lindy didn't call that night until ten o'clock. Her father had delivered her a long lecture about keeping out of other people's affairs and being responsible for what you say. Finally she had persuaded him to read the editorial. "He had to admit," she said, laughing a little shakily, "that he might have done the same thing himself, if he hadn't known better."

So all of us had an unexpected three-day holiday in the middle of the week, and the next morning, as I was eating a leisurely breakfast, Keith called to say that his father had given him some "twofers."

"What are twofers?"

"Ticket coupons, so you can buy two for the price of one," he explained. "There's this musical that's closing. It's not the Met, but it's on Broadway. Can you make it tomorrow afternoon?"

"Sure," I said. "My folks are taking things real well."

"I'm going to call Lindy, too," he said. "Just keep all your relatives healthy, okay?"

"It doesn't quite seem right," Mom said. "You kids are being punished. You're not supposed to be out having fun."

"Just call it cultural enrichment," I suggested. "We'll try not to enjoy ourselves too much."

It didn't take me long to get ready, but I felt pretty enough as I stood before the bureau, brushing my hair with long, even strokes. I was ready for an adventure in the city with Lindy and Keith, and I felt a little taller and older. Today there would be no grown-up with us to make sure we caught the right bus and reached the theater by curtain time. Today we were the grown-ups.

It was strange to remember that I had attended Karen's party only a few short weeks ago. Tingling with excitement and apprehension, I had labored over my appearance as though the smallest flaw would somehow ruin my chance to have a good time. Today I knew that we would all have fun, even if the show was a flop. Keith and Lindy would whisper vivid descriptions of the passersby. We would wander the streets of Manhattan munching roasted chestnuts, getting lost, finding our way again. With Keith and Lindy to share it all, it would be a memorable afternoon.

I set down my brush and fastened back my hair. I wondered where Miss Kellogg was at that moment. I thought of what she had said to me that afternoon when I poured out my despair of ever finding a place for myself at Ridge View High. "Each of us marches to the beat of a different drummer." Keith and Lindy and I had found a drummer that suited us, and had marched out of Mr. Wallace's office into a glorious three-day suspension.

The doorbell rang. I dashed downstairs and found them waiting on the front porch. "You ready?" Keith asked. "Hey, guess what! It's snowing!"

I slipped my arm through Lindy's and stepped down to the sidewalk. Snowflakes pattered against my face, light and fast. "It's snowing!" I repeated. I tilted my face up and caught a flake on the tip of my nose.

Keith hummed a few preliminary notes and burst into a cascade of song. The singing filled the quiet street, proclaiming that it was a very special afternoon.

"Come on," Lindy protested. "Sing something we know, or else teach us something!"

"How about a round?" he suggested. He began, "Come, follow follow follow, follow follow follow me. . . ."

"Once more, slower," I said. "I want to get the tune."

After he had sung it through the second time, Lindy and I struggled with the melody, making mistakes, but singing it through from start to finish. We were about to try again when Keith cried, "Look! Here comes the bus!"

He caught my free hand and, linked in a chain across the sidewalk, we broke into a run.

Deborah Kent was born in Glen Ridge, New Jersey, and grew up in nearby Little Falls. Like Meg in *Belonging*, she studied at special Braille classes during her grade school years and then attended public high school. She was graduated from Oberlin College and received a masters in social work from Smith College. For four years Ms. Kent was a social worker at University Settlement House on New York's Lower East Side.

For the past two years she has been living and writing in San Miguel de Allende, Mexico, where there is a large colony of writers and artists. She is currently teaching blind children in San Miguel and working on a second novel; in addition, she writes a column for *Disabled: USA*, a publication of the President's Committee on Employment of the Handicapped.